A NECESSARY WITCH

A NECESSARY WITCH

SCHOOL OF NECESSARY MAGIC RAINE CAMPBELL™
BOOK 09

JUDITH BERENS   MARTHA CARR   MICHAEL ANDERLE

This book is a work of fiction.
All of the characters, organizations, and events portrayed in this novel are either products of the author's imagination or are used fictitiously. Sometimes both.

Copyright © 2019 Judith Berens, Martha Carr and Michael Anderle
Cover by Fantasy Book Design
Cover copyright © LMBPN Publishing
A Michael Anderle Production

LMBPN Publishing supports the right to free expression and the value of copyright. The purpose of copyright is to encourage writers and artists to produce the creative works that enrich our culture.

The distribution of this book without permission is a theft of the author's intellectual property. If you would like permission to use material from the book (other than for review purposes), please contact support@lmbpn.com. Thank you for your support of the author's rights.

LMBPN Publishing
PMB 196, 2540 South Maryland Pkwy
Las Vegas, NV 89109

First US edition, July 2019
Print ISBN: 978-1-64202-366-4

The Oriceran Universe (and what happens within / characters / situations / worlds) are Copyright © 2017-19 by Martha Carr and LMBPN Publishing.

A NECESSARY WITCH TEAM

Thanks to the JIT Readers

Daniel Weigert
Shari Regan
Jeff Goode
Dave Hicks
Jeff Eaton
Dorothy Lloyd
Micky Cocker
Diane L. Smith
Misty Roa
Larry Omans

If we've missed anyone, please let us know!

Editor
The Skyhunter Editing Team

DEDICATIONS

From Martha

To everyone who still believes in magic
and all the possibilities that holds.
To all the readers who make this
entire ride so much fun.
And to my son, Louie and so many wonderful friends who
remind me all the time of what
really matters and how wonderful
life can be in any given moment.

From Michael

To Family, Friends and
Those Who Love
To Read.
May We All Enjoy Grace
To Live The Life We Are
Called.

CHAPTER ONE

Raine smiled as she stepped off the jitney, her suitcase in hand, and paused to allow the crush of students in front of her to move ahead. The circle drive had obviously been cleared recently, but a decent layer of snow smothered the grounds compared to last year. She'd read it had been colder than usual in Charlottesville that winter, which explained the substantial snowfalls, both in town and at the school. Last winter had been far more disappointing in that regard.

She extended the handle on her rolling suitcase and strolled toward the main doors of the mansion. Her breath emerged in short, visible puffs. Living in Virginia most of the year made her less resistant to cold, but the mild chill in the air wasn't enough to challenge her. Instead, it brought a smile to her face as she slowed and searched the faces of the other students who milled about the entrance and chatted. Some, she barely knew. Others, such as Juniper, she'd spent the last four years with as classmates.

The black-haired girl waved to her and she returned the

greeting. Juniper returned to her conversation with another girl. Raine had never been close to her, although they maintained a friendly relationship. She didn't mind as she had a group of close friends. It wasn't possible for anyone to be close to everyone else.

A small trace of melancholy slipped in with her musings on friendship. This was the spring semester of their senior year. They'd learned together, loved together, and fought together, and these would be the last months for the FBI Trouble Squad. It might be too much to declare it the end of an era, but it felt that way.

Raine walked toward the doors of the mansion, her thoughts on the coming graduation. There were so many opportunities awaiting them all in the future so she didn't mind graduating, but she also understood that her time at the School of Necessary Magic would be precious for the rest of her life. Her experience had transformed her from merely another FBI agent wannabe to a witch with great and deep friendships and practical experience fighting evil.

Should they try to make the last semester special? She wasn't sure. Everything she did with her friends felt special, whether it was movie nights or a trip to the kemana. There was no grand experience missing, nothing she had been dying to do and had put off. After so many semesters of adventure, she would have been happy if there was no strange occurrence and no deadly mystery to threaten anyone she cared about.

She sighed as she stepped inside the building and headed toward the grand staircase. Cina, the leader of the Children of Thoth, had escaped the Ruby Falls police during their last encounter. Raine had disrupted her plan to kidnap Madelyn, but the woman might still be out there, waiting for her next chance to snatch the poor girl and use her as part of a twisted ritual.

Common sense would suggest the witch priestess was far away from Ruby Falls, if not in a different country. Wanted criminals tended to avoid the places where they were well-known, but that might not be the case with Cina. Her obsession with and rants about Madelyn being the key to her plan to somehow gain access to so-called primordial magic meant the risk she posed would remain until she was apprehended.

Raine shook her head as she approached her dorm room. Madelyn would be safe. Everyone knew the risk now, from the professors to the PDA, and it wasn't like the PDA had flooded the area with agents. They must not have thought it was a big risk.

The Coral Elf would enjoy school life as she learned not only magic but what it meant to be alive. While the authorities might not know what to do with her in the future, they had a few years to figure it out.

And if necessary, the FBI Trouble Squad would be there to protect her as they always were for everyone who needed the help.

She opened the door to their room. None of her friends had arrived yet. That gave her time to check on a little something.

Raine trudged through the snow on her way toward the

stables. It didn't take long until she spotted blue amongst all the white.

Madelyn skated across a perfectly oval sheet of ice near the stables, a bright smile on her face. She jumped and executed a beautiful spin before she landed with ease and extended her leg.

The girl waved to her as she approached. "Hello, Raine. Welcome back."

"Hi. It's good to be back." She gestured to the ice. "Another Dorvu ice rink?" She looked around for the silver dragon, but he wasn't there.

The elf shook her head. "With all the snow on the ground already, it was easy for me to do it myself. I don't always want to bother him." She waggled her fingers clad in wool gloves. "The more I accept that I'm a Coral Elf, the easier water and ice magic is for me. I can do a lot that… um, natural-born Coral Elves can't do easily, but that doesn't change the basic strength or natural abilities."

Raine nodded, happy that Madelyn hadn't fallen back into her old habit of referring to herself in demeaning ways such as fake or unreal. "How was your break? Did you have fun?"

"Good," Madelyn replied. "I did a lot of reading and skating." She stopped at the edge of her ice rink and tipped one of her skates forward. "They still don't want me to leave the school grounds because of the Thothites, but I don't mind. It's no big deal."

"Are you sure you don't mind? I would understand if you found it frustrating."

"No. Cina is dangerous, and I won't let her reach me. The PDA, FBI, or the police will catch her. I still have so much to learn, and it's not like I need to go into Ruby Falls or Charlottesville." Her expression brightened. "And now everyone's back to school, including you all and Erin."

Madelyn had saved Erin last Halloween from a spirit, and they'd become fast friends. Raine was glad to see it. Given their different grade levels and the existing relationships between the FBI Trouble Squad, it could be hard for other people to always socialize comfortably with them, even though they tried to make people feel welcome. It was better for the girl to have a friend closer to her grade level. For the most part, she chatted with the Trouble Squad on occasion and came to movies nights, but toward the end of the semester, she took most of her meals with Erin rather than Raine and her posse.

"That's good to hear," she said.

The Coral Elf gasped. "I almost forgot to tell you. I found out from the headmistress that Erin will move in with me. She said it was time that I got used to living with someone other than my sister, and Erin asked about it. I don't know if she only likes the idea of having one roommate, but I don't mind either way." She nodded, a determined look on her face. "And the headmistress is right. It'll be strange staying with anyone else but Vianna, but this is also part of moving on, right?"

"Yes, it is." Raine shrugged. "I had to move in with Uncle Jerry, so I know what it's like to lose a loved one and then have to change your living conditions. Plus, Erin can help you more with social skills and that kind of thing." She frowned. "I only wish you weren't still stuck on the grounds. I worried about it when I was on vacation, but I guess it's silly when I think about it now."

Madelyn looked confused. "Worried about me being on the grounds?"

"No, about Cina. I know it's silly because most of the professors stay here over the break, but after everything that happened with the Chaos Witch, I was a little nervous. But you're safe, and it's not like the PDA is even here." She shrugged.

"It's okay." The girl waved a hand airily. "If Cina could get into the school, she would have tried during the break because there were fewer people around, and she didn't, which means she can't." She shrugged, hope in her eyes. "All I have to do is wait until she is caught, then it'll be fine."

Raine sighed and nodded. "I know. It simply annoys me. I guess that's what is really getting me. She's the criminal, but it's like they have you under house arrest."

Madelyn shook her head. "You have to understand how grateful I am to the headmistress and the others here."

"Grateful?"

"Yes, grateful." She looked down, her pale cheeks scarlet-touched by the weather. "Vianna and I…we used to be Maeve, and we did bad things. Then, when Maeve became us, we lied about who we were. Headmistress Berens had all the reasons in the world to send us off with the PDA, and Agent Oliver could have insisted that I go with her. Vianna always thought if we trusted anyone, we would end up in some warded cell to be poked and prodded." She sighed. "But it didn't work out that way. When we finally trusted everyone…" She blinked her glistening eyes. "I sometimes wonder if we'd trusted people sooner, maybe she wouldn't have died."

Raine headed over to hug her. "It's okay, Madelyn. The important thing is that you're here now, and you trust us and the professors. Everyone will protect you."

"I know," she whispered. She smiled, pulled away, and wiped a tear on her sleeve. "And I protected Erin, but that's not enough. I want to be strong enough so I can help people like you do. Like you'll continue to do as an FBI agent."

"Thanks. That means a lot." Raine rubbed her hands together. "I don't have my gloves or wand so I think I'll head back in. If you need anything, you know where to find me." She waved and turned back toward the school.

A role model and inspiration. It had never been her intent to be either to Madelyn. She only wanted to be her friend, but she couldn't deny how happy she felt.

CHAPTER TWO

Raine was almost back to the mansion when someone stepped in front of her. She blinked and stepped back. "Sorry, I wasn't paying—" She rolled her eyes once she saw who it was. "You could have called out to me, Cameron. I almost walked right into you."

He stood there wearing a lop-sided grin with no hint of shame and shrugged. "You were making your overthinking face. It was too much fun to try to surprise you. It knocks those obsessions right out and resets the old Campbell brain from that mode."

"I wasn't overthinking." She looked to the side to avoid his gaze. "Okay. Maybe a little. Like ten percent. But if I always do that, isn't it normal thinking for me and not overthinking?"

"You're right. You wouldn't be you if you weren't worrying too much about something." The shifter gestured around. "Nice snow. It's kind of relaxing. Do you want to go for a little walk? I love the smell of the air here right now. It smells so fresh. Sometimes, I like it more than home."

Raine lifted her hands. "No gloves and I forgot my wand. I've gone native Virginian and I'm starting to get too cold. I've been out here a while. I went to find and chat to Madelyn."

Cameron dug into the pockets of his puffy blue jacket and pulled out a pair of black gloves. He handed them to her. "I don't need any. Maybe my shifter instincts anticipated that you would need them. I've been looking for you. I really wanted to talk to you about something."

She slipped the gloves on and took his offered arm. "It hasn't exactly been that long since we last saw each other. I don't think I'm *that* irresistible." She winked.

"Are you so sure?" He grinned. "Is this the part where I say something like, 'Even five minutes is too long since I've last seen you?'"

"I don't think I have a big enough ego to believe that." Raine laughed. "Not that I mind hearing it."

They trudged along until they reached a well-worn path where the footprints of dozens of other students had packed the snow down. A maze of flattened snow lay between the interconnected paths, even though the untrampled snow wasn't a serious threat unless a student wore flipflops.

"I have a confession," Cameron said finally. "A big one."

Raine glanced at him. "Confession?" Given his facial expression, she doubted he was about to admit anything terrible. He looked more excited than worried.

"Maybe it's more an admission." He frowned a little but the slight smile lingered. "You're not the only one who can overthink, you know. I started thinking when I returned home after staying with you. William and some of the pack chatted one day about the future, and that set me off. I know we've talked about it a few times, but I didn't have a good answer at first."

"Were they mad at you?"

He shook his head. "No one cares much. As far as the pack is concerned, I can stay with them for as long as I need to make the right decisions, but that wasn't good enough for me."

She sighed. "I hope you're not still upset about not having everything mapped out right away. You don't have to."

"But that's just it. I do." He pointed to the school. "This place has done me so much good, but part of the problem is that it's a magic school and I'm a shifter. We're products of magic, but we can't do magic. When you can't do spells, it makes you think your talents aren't as useful for different kinds of jobs. I keep going round and round, thinking about the military, police, and those kinds of careers because I'm a shifter who has spent time studying military history. But I'm not like you, Raine. I'm not obsessed with learning new things, and it's not like I have the kind of art skills or management skills some of our friends do."

"That doesn't mean—"

"It's not what you think," Cameron interrupted. "This isn't a bad thing. I'm not here to talk about how worried I am or about being behind you because I now know what I'll do. The clear direction is all I needed."

"You know what you'll do now?"

"I do. And I thought long and hard about it too. I like the idea of being a police officer, but I'm not as into investigation as you. We've talked about that already. I'm a protector. That's at the heart of what I should do, so I need a job that involves that. I thought about being a bodyguard, but I'd have to work for somebody, and I don't want to be some guy who protects someone simply for money. That's not good enough."

Raine nodded. "I can understand that, but you came up with something else that works?"

A huge grin split his face. "Secret Service."

"Secret Service?" She walked in silence and considered that for a moment.

"I'm not sure I can get in, but it's a job that's part investigation but heavy on protection. I know that being Secret Service doesn't always mean protecting the president or congressmen, but it'll still be a major part of what I do, and it's a job I can feel good about." He stopped and released her arm. "It's not only that, but it's important. If I can get in, I'll be a shifter doing all that, not simply another magical." He sighed. "The dark wizards spent so much time spreading rumors about shifters that most people still don't trust us, and this will help with that. We still live in a country where they have bounty hunters hunting magical criminals, and I know what people say away from school. Half the country still thinks shifters change under full moons and attack people."

Raine nodded. "I'm sure we can get recommendations to help you from both Agent Connor and Agent Oliver, let alone the professors. It has to mean something if FBI and PDA agents have a good opinion of you. I wouldn't have thought of it, but now you mention it, I think it's perfect. And you're sure?"

Cameron responded with a firm nod. "I'm surer about this than I have been about anything in a long time other than you."

She blushed and turned away. "That's good. Do you think you'll be able to get special dispensation to join early like I have for the FBI?"

He shook his head. "I don't know, but I don't want that."

Raine wrinkled her forehead in confusion. "You don't?"

"Nope. I want to be a symbol as a shifter in the Secret Service, at least one that's honest about what they are. I'm sure they've had others in the past no one knew about, but if I do this, I need to do everything normally so no one will ever question how I got in. Because you know people will, and dark wizards will whisper in their ears to tell them they are right to do it because no one's supposed to trust a shifter." He uttered a low growl of frustration. "No. I'll go to college and then join them."

"Have you heard from the schools you applied to yet?" she asked.

Cameron nodded and some of the anger faded from his face. "They all accepted me already, and since I want to be Secret Service, I thought I should start getting used to D.C. This is as good a time as any to tell you I'll go to Georgetown. Now that I know what I want to do, I also know what I want to study—criminology. You'll have a few years of experience under your belt when I start, so I'll be still behind, but it's all good."

"Behind?" She shook her head. "It's not like that. It isn't a competition."

"I know. I'm not worried. For the first time in a long time, I'm not worried." He smiled and cupped her cheek. "You're shivering too much. Let's get you inside."

Raine didn't resist as he took her arm again and turned. She hadn't wanted to admit to Cameron that she was worried about him. Supporting him until he could decide what he wanted to do was the only thing she could do. Her future was so clear, and she didn't want to risk letting her own selfish desires push her boyfriend onto the wrong path for him. Now, they could both go into the future together, confident in their choices.

Her heart rate kicked up. It would be a great last semester.

CHAPTER THREE

There really was nothing quite like pixie food. Raine all but inhaled her spaghetti noodles in the dining hall where she sat with her friends for their first meal of the semester. The current discussion had drifted to people's college acceptances, and Cameron had announced his decision along with his Secret Service plans.

Philip grinned and bowed over his arm. "Ladies and gentlemen, I'll let you know that I'll go to Yale. There are many opportunities there for me to do internships at NGOs and charities during my breaks, too, so it'll be an easy transition from college to what I want to do with my life."

"Straight to the FBI Academy for me," Raine said with a shrug. "But that's not news to you guys." She glanced at William. He'd made it clear last semester he didn't want a special dispensation, but she wondered if he had changed his mind.

The half-Ifrit swallowed a sip of his orange juice and set it down. "I settled on the University of Virginia."

"As in…you know, the one not that far away?"

He smiled. "Yes. It'll feel weird not being at this school but so close. I really liked the university when we've visited. At least I'll be close to Cameron. I'll study criminology like him, too, so we'll have to get together and compare notes on our programs." He turned his attention toward Adrien.

The elf boy shook his head. "An advanced education can have its value, but most Guardian training is focused around an apprenticeship model. My parents originally sent my brother and me here to both help refine our magic while also making sure we were exposed to different kinds of magicals in a foreign culture. They thought it would help us become more flexible."

Raine nodded. "Do you think it worked?"

Adrien smirked. "I don't know. Do you?"

"You're way more laid back than when we first met you," Philip said. "But you're not the only one doing an apprenticeship." His gaze slid to Evie.

She smiled warmly. "I've asked Professor Fowler to help me with some final big projects here because I'll go straight from school to the apprenticeship. Everything's been worked out. What about you, Sara? When we talked about it right before we went on break, you said you weren't sure if you would go to art school or if you would start your own studio right away."

Sara nodded, an excited look on her face. "I talked it over with my family." She shook her head, and surprise replaced the excitement. "It's funny how supportive they are of me now. After all the trouble they gave me over my magic, I honestly thought they wouldn't want me to go into art, let alone support me so much."

"And what did you all decide?" Evie asked.

"I'll go to art school." The kitsune nodded firmly. "I've already received two acceptances out of the three places where I applied. The third school hasn't replied yet, but it doesn't matter because my number one choice already accepted me."

"That's the School of the Art Institute of Chicago, right?" Raine asked when she recalled a few brief discussions last semester on the subject.

"Yes. I love my art, but I know I still have a long way to go with my fundamentals. Spending some time with a broad spectrum of instruction from varying backgrounds will help."

"Didn't you say they had a Magic in Art minor there?" Raine frowned, not sure if she remembered correctly or had simply confused some stray facts from books or articles she'd read over the break. Sometimes, it could get confusing.

Sara clasped her hands together, her face aglow with delight. "They do. They are one of the few art schools with a program that has almost twenty years of experience, too. It turns out there was a witch and wizard on the faculty back when the gates started opening, so they immediately started integrating magic into the art programs there. It's not only magicals adding spells to their art either. They also have magicals and non-magicals work together on different projects, too. It's all about collaboration for maximum creativity."

"That sounds great." Raine tried to twirl more noodles

on her fork, but she'd already cleared her plate. The inevitable result of delicious pixie meals.

"It's kind of strange," Philip said with a slight frown.

"What is?" She looked around. There was nothing unusual in the dining hall. Pixies fluttered around to inspect some of the tables while they chatted with the witches, wizards, elves, and others who attended the school. Nothing stood out at all.

He nodded toward Sara. "Her school has a program with magic, but it's not the same thing as a magical college." He gestured around the dining hall. "This is a magical school that was started after the gates started to open, and places like Orono became true magical schools when they were semi-magical schools before, but there aren't any real magical colleges on Earth."

The kitsune shook her head. "It's not the same thing. By the time someone's ready to go to college, they have control over their magic. It's probably not necessary."

"She's right," Raine said. "We learn spells and potions and that kind of thing here, but if there were less risk of accident and people freaking out, I'm sure they would simply integrate magicals into regular schools as they do in places like the FBI."

Adrien frowned. "I think I prefer this arrangement. Being a magical brings with it certain specific needs that can't easily be matched in a conventional school without causing too much disruption to both the magicals and non-magicals."

She shrugged. "Maybe, but the fact that magicals aren't yelling for special all-magical colleges proves that it's not as much of an issue."

Evie finished the last bite of her fruit salad. "Do you think magical schools like this one will go away in the future?"

"Maybe but probably not. The safety issue will always be important, but I do think it means magical colleges won't ever become common. They simply don't have a strong reason to exist, and I think that's a good thing."

Cameron frowned. "A good thing? Why?"

"Because the fewer barriers between magicals and non-magicals, the better." Raine sighed. "It shouldn't have been a big deal when my power manifested, but it was. I almost thought I was originally in trouble. In the back of my mind, I half-wondered if this was like the equivalent of a magical school for troubled kids or something."

The Light Elf scoffed. "This is one of the best magic schools in the world. My parents wouldn't have sent me here otherwise."

"I know. I know. It was only a brief thought. It helped that so many people made it clear that it something very different, and given the attitude of certain annoying students when I got here, I quickly realized it was more like a fancy prep school than anything." She released a wistful sigh. "And now, it's coming to an end."

Philip made a face. "When you say it like that, it's so depressing."

Raine shook her head. "It doesn't have to be. We've all grown up here." She smiled at Cameron. "We've all found people we love, found ourselves, and helped others. I won't say I won't miss this place or seeing you all every day after we graduate, but I'm also ready to move on to the next chapter of my life."

Adrien responded with a curt nod. "I have unfinished business in that I need to lead the team to a championship, but I'm ready to graduate, too. We've fought evil together as the Trouble Squad, but I want to do it as a proper Guardian."

"I look forward to my apprenticeship," Evie said. "All potions, all the time."

Sara exhaled a contented sigh. "And I look forward to being able to focus more on my art."

Cameron grinned at Raine. "I have to hurry and get my degree so I can save the president from crazy chaos witches."

"When I came to this school," William began, "I didn't feel good about myself. I felt angry about my family situation but now, I'm at peace, and I know I'll be able to easily visit Evie on the weekends. I'm ready for the future, too."

Philip gave a solemn nod. "I get it. We've helped a lot of people at this school. Now, it's time to take our problem solving to the rest of the world."

"Exactly," Raine said. "The future is coming for all of us, and it might make us uneasy at times, but that doesn't mean it's not bright and full of hope at the end of the path."

CHAPTER FOUR

Adrien folded his arms over his chest and stood against the wall of the cramped library study room. Seven other students filled the room—the other members of the Louper team—and it didn't help that several, such as Dennis, weren't all that small. A few people found chairs, but that left the students jammed together in an area meant to fit half as many people.

A little discomfort wasn't bad. It was good even though this was the first Louper meeting of the semester. He didn't want the team too relaxed. If they no longer hungered for the win, they would become lazy and make mistakes, and the season would slip through their fingers. He was proud of their performance last year, but he was determined to bring home the championship. With the finals closing in, they needed to keep the fire burning inside each player.

"Why are we all crammed in here?" Dennis asked and his gaze flicked to a pile of books on the small table in the center of the room. "We all show up for today's Louper practice and you bring us to the library. It's hard to play

Louper in the library. It's hard to even practice in the library, let alone some tiny little room where we can't even all read books together without stomping on each other's feet."

The others nodded. Some seemed annoyed but most were confused.

"Louper's evolved over the years, and it'll continue to evolve. That's the nature of the game." Adrien pointed at the books. "I've been happy with your practices so far, and I think we're ready for the game coming up. And so, if we want to win a championship this season, we'll need to make sure we evolve with it. A team that spends too much time satisfied with their strategy will find their opponents adapt to it easily. Also, a team that doesn't understand how the game has changed won't even be able to develop a decent strategy to annoy their opponents."

"What does that mean?" Hilda asked with a frown. "Are those books on the history of Louper? That's all very inspirational and stuff, but haven't we already built on all the old strategies and tips and tricks?"

"No. You don't understand. This isn't about the history of Louper." The captain shook his head. "To be clear, we have a good team. You've all come into your own, and I believe this is a team I can lead all the way to a championship, but that's only true if we account for our weaknesses. We have good mobility, good flexibility, good stamina, and good technique." He offered them a small smile. "And we're one of the bravest teams in the league, but getting that token in Louper can come down to seconds. Anything that slows us down can cost us a match and has in the past."

Several players frowned.

Adrien held his palm up. "Let me be clear on this point. As team captain, that is my fault, not yours. I should identify and take care of team weaknesses through training or strategy, so our existing weaknesses are a reflection of holes in my leadership skills."

"So you want to do speed drills or something?" Carlos asked. "Is that what those books are? References about speed magic? You didn't need to bring us to the library to tell us about that."

Dennis grunted. "I'm fast enough already."

"No one's ever fast enough, not until you're always faster than others." The elf scoffed. "But if it were only about improving our magic, I'd integrate it into the drills we already do. No, this is about the increasing number of non-maze puzzles directly integrated into matches, especially over the last few seasons. Everything I've heard suggests that will only increase this semester and going forward. The league wants Louper to reflect the best aspects of students, physical and mental, and that is one way to implement it. They also feel it will expand interest in the game if it's not as purely battle-focused."

"Puzzles aren't a big deal." Dennis shrugged. "We've handled them fine in the past."

Jackson sighed. "If they weren't a big deal, we wouldn't have ended up with the other teams so close to the token last semester."

Adrien nodded. "Exactly. Louper is, fundamentally, a race, and the league might want to balance things out in different ways, but I don't care about balance. I care about winning."

"I don't get it," Dennis said. "If we've been close but still win, doesn't that mean we're doing fine?"

The captain shook his head. "No. We don't want to do as well as our opponents. We need to do better—far better. We should solve puzzles faster so it's not even close and doesn't come down to seconds." He nodded again to the book pile. "And that's where those books come in. They are all about puzzles and mental challenges of various types. From what we've seen in the matches, the league doesn't want to stump us too hard, but they also don't want to make things too focused on any particular type of mindset. The more we study different types of puzzles, the better prepared we'll be. Keep in mind that they're doing this at the pro levels as well. Did anyone watch the match between Portland and LA?"

Irina made a face. "You're talking about the student riddle, aren't you?" She groaned.

Adrien nodded. "Yes, a simple riddle changed the course of that match. Everyone expected Portland to win, especially given how they've dominated much of the league this season. Also note that the match officials split the difference with the riddle. Getting the answer wrong released more monsters in that case. Even though Portland handled them without too much trouble, they lost time, which is why LA took the match. LA didn't even need to have some epic showdown with them. They had all the time they needed to find the token and win. A blowout." He curled his hand into a fist. "I want to give the team the championship this season, but I can't do it alone. I need your help. That means continuing to train hard and putting in extra hours, and it also means we'll all take these puzzle- and problem-solving books and read them as well. In a Louper match, a minute can be a lifetime. If we lose because of our minds instead of our magic, it'll be seriously embarrassing."

Dennis grumbled under his breath, but others, including Irina, Hilda, and Carlos looked excited. The others' faces evidenced mixed feelings.

"We've come close before to taking it all," the elf said. "We even got a little cocky because we thought we would have a perfect season, and we might very well have that this year. But even if we lose a match or two, we can still go to the championship, and when we get there, I want to destroy the other team. I want it to be boring for the spectators because of how lopsided our victory is. Honestly, if I can do that by answering a riddle faster, then we'll do exactly that." He offered them a feral grin. "We're the Cardinals, and we'll destroy anyone who stands in our way."

"Okay, when you put it that way, I'm on board," Dennis bellowed. "Yeah, Adrien. I get it now. Bring on the puzzles. Time for the Cardinals to take out the competition!"

"Bring on the puzzles!" shouted the rest of the team.

Someone rapped loudly on the door. Adrien opened it. Head Librarian Decker stood on the other side, frowned, and tapped his foot. The poppy on his bowler hat growled loudly.

"This is a library, not a Louper field," the gnome said with a slight frown. "If you have a meeting here, you need to keep it down."

"Bring on the puzzles," everyone whispered in unison.

The head librarian looked from one student to the

other with a confused frown before he shrugged. "As long as you keep it quiet." He closed the door.

"Put your work in," Adrien said, "and I'll lead you to victory."

There was another knock. He sighed and opened it.

This time, it was Raine.

"Adrien, you need to come with me," she said. "The headmistress wants to talk to us."

He frowned and nodded. "Fine." He turned to the team. "The rest of you grab one of those books. Spend at least an hour a day studying it. I don't care how you find the time, but find it."

CHAPTER FIVE

Raine tried not to sigh. They'd only been in school a couple of weeks and they hadn't been involved in anything strange or dangerous. None of them had even gone to the kemana or into town yet, so she didn't understand why the entire FBI Trouble Squad, along with Madelyn, had been summoned to Headmistress Berens' office. She had even more trouble understanding why Agent Oliver stood off to the side, while Agent Connor wasn't there.

The headmistress offered them a polite nod. At least she didn't look mad. That was promising.

Madelyn looked at the ground and rubbed her wrist. She shuffled her feet, her nervousness and discomfort apparent.

"Thank you for coming," Headmistress Berens said. "The first thing I want to make very clear is that none of you are in any trouble."

Philip and Madelyn exhaled sighs of relief. The others looked surprised, except for Adrien, who'd kept the same bland, flat expression on his face since his arrival in the room.

Raine nodded. "That's good to hear, but I don't understand why we're here. The only thing we heard is that we all needed to come to talk to you as soon as possible." Her heart pounded harder. The Coral Elf's presence suggested one disturbing possibility, but she hoped that wasn't the case for the girl's sake.

The headmistress sighed. "The PDA is deeply concerned about what happened in Ruby Falls with the Thothites. They've helped monitor the group for a while, but this was the first time they've done something so blatantly dangerous. Their actions represent a clear and menacing escalation."

"You won't force Madelyn to leave, will you?" she asked. "You might not care what students have to say on this, but we've spent a lot of time with her, and she's made great progress here. Taking her to some PDA building won't help her grow as a person."

Headmistress Berens lifted a hand and shook her head. "Calm down, Raine. No one has any intention of taking Madelyn away from the School of Necessary Magic."

She stepped back, her arms still folded. While she didn't like to be so aggressive, she had promised Vianna to help protect Madelyn. What kind of FBI agent would she be if she couldn't keep her promises to a dying girl?

Agent Oliver frowned and stepped forward. "Indeed. The last thing the PDA wants is Madelyn transferred from this school. Unfortunately, there are still many unanswered questions, and until we catch Cina, Madelyn remains a target. We know what the woman claimed she was trying to accomplish, but we have little idea of how she intends to do so. And more to the point, we know that whatever she wants will likely result in...injury to Madelyn."

The Coral Elf girl nodded reluctantly and kept her gaze focused on the ground.

Raine didn't frown, even though she wanted to. It wasn't the headmistress or Agent Oliver's fault, and getting angry with them wouldn't help. They were trying to help, but that thought didn't dull her frustration. How long would Madelyn have to live a restricted life because of some insane witch?

"Despite the fact that various legal questions remain as yet unanswered about Madelyn," the agent continued, "the PDA definitely won't sit by while a rogue witch terrorizes students. At this point, the agency isn't one hundred percent convinced that Cina is stupid enough to stay in the area after she committed such a high-profile crime. Still, given what you students have told us about what she said, we can't ignore the possibility that she will target Madelyn again, and some bureaucratic obstacles have been hurdled to enable us to actively step in. That's why I'm here. We thought, given your students' involvement with both Madelyn and Cina, that it would best to brief all of you fully so everyone is on the same page."

Cameron frowned. "And you can't simply track her or something? She might be powerful, but she's only one witch, and she doesn't even have her full special powers by her own admission."

Agent Oliver shook her head. "We've made extensive efforts to track her. Through either superior technique or the suspected artifact pendant she wears, we cannot track her directly, either with simple spells or more cumbersome directional spells. She also has almost no electronic presence in the greater world. We've reached out to the FBI to help in that regard, but at this point, she might as well not exist."

The shifter growled. "Great. Wonderful."

"If she's this hidden, it means she knows what she's doing, and she'll undoubtedly take advantage of that to launch surprise attacks." Agent Oliver pointed at Madelyn. "Cina had her chance, but she failed, which gives us an opportunity. Given their normal duties, the Ruby Falls police don't have the resources or time to divert much to the investigation of someone who might not even be there, but they are providing logistical support for the PDA. No matter what, we will not let the witch harm that girl."

Raine nodded. "Neither will we. I know we screwed up before by not immediately going to the headmistress and we won't let that happen again, but if there's anything we can do to protect her, we will."

Her friends all nodded in agreement. Cameron's eyes flashed yellow.

Headmistress Berens shook her head. "I'm happy to see that you're willing to defend your friend and I appreciate the fact that you've learned the appropriate lessons from your previous encounter. However, if we all handle this situation appropriately, you won't have to get involved at all. It's a failure of this school and law enforcement that one of our students could be targeted by Cina, to begin with." She sighed. "Unfortunately, this means we'll continue to restrict Madelyn to the school grounds for her safety. Cina might be powerful, but she doesn't demonstrate unusual magic beyond casting technique, unlike Eris. This means she has limited ability to defeat our wards, and we have every reason to believe Madelyn will be safe on school grounds. That, in turn, will give the PDA the time needed to complete their investigation."

"Agent Oliver isn't only here to guard Madelyn?" Raine asked.

The PDA agent pushed her glasses up her nose. "Although several agents are working on investigating the Thothites, there are two agents who have been assigned directly to this area, with me being one of them. My main role is to bolster school defenses. You can consider that guarding Madelyn, if you will, but I won't follow her around. She has enough stress without having a PDA agent dogging her every last step."

"T-thank you," Madelyn murmured. "For both helping and not crowding me."

"You're welcome." The woman nodded. "My partner on this case, Agent Clemson, is in the kemana doing a lower-level people-focused investigation and looking for anything or anyone who might be related to the Thothites. I would have preferred it if the agency had sent more agents to the area directly, but they are working a number of different angles in regard to the Thothites, in addition to reaching out to our sister agencies all over the world. These cultists were troublemakers in the past, so it's perhaps not surprising they are troublemakers now. But they've made their move already, and although we can't be certain of their manpower, it's obvious they suffered major losses during the last incident."

"For now, we merely wanted you to be aware of all

that," Headmistress Berens said. "It's also entirely possible that Cina is hiding on Oriceran at this point. I wish I could offer you some guarantee as to when this will all be over, but I can't. It might be next week, or it could take all semester. I'm sorry, Madelyn."

The girl sighed. "I-it's okay. I'm happy that everyone is helping me." She forced a smile. "I like it here, and I'll have a good time even if I never leave campus."

"A good attitude. For now, you may all go. If you learn of anything that might help Agent Oliver or her partner, let us know immediately."

The Trouble Squad all nodded their agreement and turned to leave. Raine nibbled on her lip and watched Madelyn as the girl trudged out of the room. She might want to have a good time that semester, but it would be hard for her to relax with a crazed witch out there obsessed with her. It was one thing when it was simply a notional threat, but Agent Oliver had crystallized it into a true nightmare.

She sighed. If there were more magicals in the FBI, the bureau could do a better job of helping with cases like this one. She couldn't wait to be an agent and help protect people.

CHAPTER SIX

With thousands of years of practice, an educated person might believe that every aspect of magic had been thoroughly cataloged, discovered, and developed and that no mysteries remained. Most of the natural magical beings of Oriceran even had the advantage of vastly longer lifespans than the typical person from Earth and even then, witches or wizards of any skill could at least wring out a few more decades for their lives and studies.

Time, therefore, wasn't an issue for magical research, but as Raine thumbed through *Ancient Magic: Truths and Myths,* her frustration built. All that time and all those long lifespans hadn't been enough to clearly establish the answer to her fundamental questions. She grunted in frustration.

As he passed, Head Librarian Decker looked at her with a grin. "Is the book being rude? I can ask it to stop."

Raine sighed. "I've tried to read up more on pure magic theory—channeling and that kind of thing. I'm not saying the professors haven't given us a good education, but it's very practical and focused on modern techniques. It's about what most people use and how they believe it works, and I keep asking myself what about everything else out there? Wizard and witch magic already works differently than, say, gnome or elf magic. That means there can be other types of magic, even if they do potentially draw on the same source."

"There can and there are." He walked over to the table and glanced down at the book. "But you're talking about something else, aren't you?"

She nodded. "We needed kemanas on Earth because the magical energy flowing from Oriceran wasn't available." She placed her palms together. "The gates were closed." She spread her palms. "And now, they're starting to open. Slowly, but they are, and magic's flowing back. Already, certain species that couldn't survive on Earth outside of kemanas are coming back. But when you think of it that way, it makes it sound like Oriceran's the source of all magic."

"It is certainly a source of magic. Whether it is the source of all magic isn't a question I think anyone mortal truly knows the answer to." Head Librarian Decker adjusted his bowler hat for a moment. His poppy remained silent. "I presume this is about the Thothites?"

"Yes. I keep wondering if Cina's right and there is some kind of primordial magic." She grimaced. "This doesn't mean I think she should be able to sacrifice Madelyn to gain access to it, and I don't think *she* should have it if she doesn't already. Still, it makes me wonder about all the things we've maybe gotten wrong about magic because everyone's made any number of assumptions simply because it works out for them, and they all ask, 'Why bother going farther?'"

"I won't claim there aren't numerous mysteries that remain unexplained about magic, but the idea that Earth had access to some kind of primordial magic doesn't make much sense, especially if Cina feels it is a separate thing from Oriceran magic entirely." The gnome shrugged. "I've been around for…a while, and I've read books from even farther back. We have tens of thousands of years of history, direct or indirect, we can look at concerning Oriceran civilization. We have decent to good information as far back as fifty thousand years and excellent information for the last ten thousand. Where was the ancient magic before? And if it's from the far distant past, why isn't there any sign? Or evidence other than the ravings of a cult? Why does the collective memory of humanity point at Oriceran? I suppose my ultimate problem is that if this thing existed, you would think someone—either on Earth or Oriceran—would have already discovered it rather than it only being somehow discovered in the middle of the twenty-first century by some weird sect."

Raine shook her head. "If the Thothites are right, they've known for a while."

"They obviously didn't have this magic before. Otherwise, they wouldn't have been forced underground or they could have convinced the magical authorities that their efforts were worthwhile."

She sighed. "I suppose. And I know Headmistress Berens thinks it's only an amulet, but Cina did all kinds of magic without a wand. That has to mean something."

"Does it?" Head Librarian Decker shrugged. "Might I

present a more prosaic explanation than primordial magic or even a powerful artifact?"

"Go ahead."

The gnome smiled and held his hand up. A glowing butterfly appeared.

She frowned a little and glanced at the magical insect. "I don't understand."

"Did I use a wand, Raine?" He smiled casually.

"No, but you're a gnome. Are you saying she's not actually a witch? Why would she recruit witch and wizard followers then?"

"I can't answer that." He lowered his hand and the butterfly disappeared. "What I'm saying is that magic is closer to science in many ways. It has patterns and rules that can be exploited. Truths, if you will. Overly complicated scenarios are less common than you might think. I'm fundamentally saying there are at least two explanations for Cina's displayed powers that don't require you to invoke some mysterious lost primordial magic." He tapped the page of the open book. "And this is the true challenge of scholarship. An open mind is necessary to find the truth, but if you have a too open mind, it's far too easy to waste time following paths that run in circles or lead far away from the truth."

"'Evidence leads the case.' Agent Connor's always telling me that." Raine rubbed her temples. "But he's also always warning me against bias and that kind of thing."

"A good warning, whether in criminal investigation or scholarship. The false prophet is often the loudest and can even be the most persuasive because they aren't burdened with the shackles and limits of actual truth." Head

Librarian Decker shook his head. "Not only that, but there's a certain arrogance afflicting all currently living and thinking beings that can prejudice them."

"Arrogance? What do you mean?"

"The belief that we live in a special and unique time."

She laughed. "But we do."

"Oh?" He raised an eyebrow in challenge. "Why do you believe that?"

Raine pointed to her wand on the table. "Magic has returned to Earth. The gates opened, and they did that not much before I was born."

He shook his head. "The gates open and the gates close. It's a known cycle. Not only that, but the gates have only begun to open. The magic available on Earth remains limited." He twirled a finger in the air and small, glowing three-dimensional images of Earth and Oriceran appeared. "Magic will stay with Earth for thousands of years, exactly as it was absent for thousands of years. So why is it that you feel this time of magic being back is special and unique when it's happened before? Not only that, it'll be less impressive in some ways than what life will be like on Earth in a thousand years."

She frowned. The gnome's logic *felt* wrong but she couldn't quite pinpoint why.

"You don't think this is a special time, maybe even a dangerous time?" she asked.

"Some do. I don't." Head Librarian Decker chuckled and his poppy blew a raspberry. "Dangerous? The Great War was dangerous. For all the commotion on Earth, there's no serious risk of a global magical war right now, or even a technological one. Danger is a relative thing. Even during the most peaceful times on Oriceran, there was struggle and strife." He smiled. "I don't say this to diminish the suffering of individuals. You will go into a job that will help you ease some of that suffering and punish those who cause it. I say all this to point out that one has to be cautious about believing they inhabit a special era."

Raine closed her book. "It doesn't matter, though, if we actually live in a unique time in history. It only matters that Cina believes it."

"Oh? Why do you say that?"

"Because that means she might still grab Madelyn. I thought it wasn't a big deal, but now that the PDA is here, it really has me worried."

He nodded slightly. "I can understand that, but the fact that they are here should leave you less worried. This isn't a situation where no one will take the threat seriously. Leave the proper authorities to handle it. You're not an FBI agent yet, and you've already done your part by saving her before. It's your last semester before you leave your last vestiges of childhood behind."

"What do you mean?"

"You'll go into the FBI Academy after school, correct?"

Raine nodded. "Yes. Agent Connor will help me with additional pre-training during the summer, but yes, I go in the fall."

The head librarian gestured around the room. "Then enjoy being a student. Enjoy being a teen girl. You should be thinking about Valentine's Day, not worrying about magical cults."

She shrugged. "I can worry about both."

The gnome laughed. "That you can." He shook his head

and a smile lingered on his face. "I'll talk to you later, Raine. But try to enjoy your last semester here."

Raine shook her head. "You don't understand."

"What?" Librarian Decker stared at her, a confused expression on his face.

"No matter what has happened. I've always enjoyed my semesters here."

"Good. Keep that attitude up, and you'll have a fulfilling life."

CHAPTER SEVEN

They'd all been busy during the first few weeks of school, so this was their first movie night. Raine settled into her space on the couch next to Cameron. It was also different because of a plan Philip had suggested at the beginning of the semester. They would abandon rotating choices for the rest of the year.

He stood in front of the DVD player, a smile on his face as he slid in the night's movie. "Everyone's still on board for the Tour De Shyamalan? Only his major movies, and we'll start with *The Sixth Sense* and work our way forward."

Madelyn popped some M&Ms into her mouth. "Does it matter that I've seen some of these? I watch many movies, even without you all." She sighed and looked down. "I'm sorry."

"Don't be sorry for that," Raine said. "It's okay for you to have your own life. We get that."

The wizard shook his head. "It doesn't matter. Some of us might have seen some of them or even all of them, but we haven't all watched his major films in order and evaluated them as a movie club. It'll be a totally different experience."

Cameron shrugged. "I still think it sounds interesting. It gets us back to our roots with having a particular theme and all."

Raine looked around the room. She'd seen a few Shyamalan movies but far from all. "I do think it's important to note that many movies have twists. I hope that's not too much of a spoiler, but we should make sure not to discuss it before watching it if we've seen it."

Philip frowned. "Good point. Who in here hasn't seen *The Sixth Sense?*"

Evie, Sara, and William raised their hands.

"Good. A decent number. That means we can have a real discussion about whether people saw the twist coming. I think this will be interesting." He grinned. "His career rose and fell and rose again. I don't think any of his stuff in the 2020s and 2030s reached the peak of some of his earlier films, and he hasn't made one this decade, but who knows? This semester will be a cinematic rollercoaster." He pressed play and walked over to take a seat beside Sara.

Everyone mostly remained quiet until the credits. They consumed more popcorn and M&Ms than usual, but most of the latter was by Madelyn. She polished off an entire bowl on her own.

Philip walked over to eject the DVD. "Okay, I'll go

ahead ask. Of the three who hadn't seen the movie before, who saw the twist coming?"

Sara shook her head. "I'll be honest. I didn't see it coming. It all makes sense after the reveal, but I really never saw it coming. I guess that makes it a good twist."

Evie licked her lips. "I suspected. Since we never see Malcolm actually communicating with her and her talking in return, it did make me wonder. It is a ghost movie, after all."

William nodded. "I knew from the beginning, actually. I think they shouldn't have put him in there getting shot right away. My thought was, 'Hey, you never see him in the hospital or anything.' Maybe I have a suspicious mind."

"I guessed correctly the first time I saw it when I was about halfway through," Raine said. "I still think it's a good movie. It's great having the twist that first time, but when you know it's coming, you can spend more time looking for the clues. Even the lighting and color is different in the ghost scenes. There are subtle clues there, and it's interesting to look for them."

Madelyn shivered. "I-I didn't see the twist coming, but I related to the movie in a different way." She sighed. "Since I'm sensitive to spirits and all, at least when the veil's thin. I'm glad I can only really see spirits on Halloween. When I watched the movie, I kept thinking how awful it would be to see spirits all the time."

Adrien frowned. "But spirits from the World in Between and the ghosts of that movie aren't exactly the same thing. Some of the movie ghosts are hostile, but they aren't as dangerous as the ones we've dealt with during the veil thinning. For one thing, Cole can solve their problems with a simple understanding of what they need and can help them move on. Arguably, he *should* solve their problems because he's been blessed with special abilities that most people around him don't have. The movie doesn't exactly explain if he's completely unique, but I doubt it, although his abilities are at least rare enough to be of use in his immediate area."

"Is that why you're going to become a Guardian?" Madelyn asked. "Because you have abilities other people don't?"

His brow raised, and he smiled. "I hadn't thought of it that way, but I suppose that's true. Light Elves aren't all that rare on Oriceran, but on Earth, we are. Even magicals are somewhat uncommon, which is why so many of us from all over are in this one school. The world might continue to grow more magical in the future, but now, everyone in this room—regardless of their attunement to spirits—is closer to Cole than we might like to think."

Raine threaded her fingers and rested her chin atop them in thought. "That's one of the first things I thought about—you know, about how my power could help other people. I was scared and surprised when my magic came in, especially since it was uncontrolled, but I already wanted to go into the FBI, so it seemed like an easy jump to go from normal woman to witch in the FBI. There are bad guys out there, magical and non-magical, and since I was blessed with these abilities, I couldn't see not using them to help others."

Sara brushed a few rogue strands of red hair out of her eyes and sighed. "I never thought of it that way. When I waited for my magic to come in, I wanted it so badly because of the way my family acted and my own expectations. But I'll be honest. I never really saw it as something I needed to use to help other people. I obviously do use it that way, but maybe I'm more selfish because I don't want to fight dark wizards or criminals."

Raine shook her head.

Philip patted her on the hand. "It's okay. Not everyone needs to be an FBI agent, Guardian, or Secret Service agent. We all do our part in our own ways. Raine's inclined that way, so her magic path is also that way. I hope to explore ways I can use my magic to help people when I'm in college and interning, but my heart's more at the organizational level than the field level. So even if I end up working for an NGO or charity or something, I hope it's more about me knowing the best way to leverage magical resources than running around in the field zapping my wand."

"I agree with Philip," Evie said. "There are different ways to help people. I went through a lot of trouble when I tried to decide if I wanted to be a healer or focus more on potions, but they both help people in their own way."

William nodded, but he remained silent. Cameron listened quietly, a slight smile on his face.

"Exactly," Raine said. "Remember, Cole didn't run around beating ghosts up in the movie. He used his abilities to help them find peace. We all have to do the best with the abilities and personalities we have. Everyone here has a future career that will help people in different ways, whether protecting them, providing for them, or nourishing them. It's not like the world can function and be a good place if everyone does the same job."

Sara smiled. "Thanks. That makes me feel better."

Philip grinned. "I never thought a classic ghost movie would lead to us talking about how our magic should be used." He chuckled. "You never know what'll happen with movie night."

CHAPTER EIGHT

Adrien rushed forward through the thick jungle foliage, his sword in hand. His eyes narrowed on a bright white flare in the distance. The dense trees blocked much of the light and the thick canopy veiled most of the sky, but the magic remained unmistakable.

He glanced over his shoulder. Carlos, Hilda, Marcus, and Irina were right behind him, their wands at the ready and determination imprinted on their faces. He'd already subbed Jackson and Dennis out after they were hurt but not eliminated.

As the captain had said many times, Louper was, at its core, a race to the token. Sometimes, the match officials made it difficult to track or find the token, and the search itself was the key to the match. At other times, they made it obvious, such as in this match where a bright golden pyramid rose above the center of the jungle-filled island, visible even through the dense vegetation. The token gleamed and glowed brightly until it resembled a small sun before it dimmed again to an invisible dot.

At least, they all assumed it was the token. If not, it was a major misdirection. The elf's years of Louper experience told him it was the goal. When the path was difficult, the target was often more obvious—another way to balance the matches—and thus far, the path had been challenging.

He gritted his teeth as the ground shuddered. "It's coming again. Everyone, get ready."

A great, yawning groan and crack echoed around them. A line of trees collapsed as swarms of colorful birds took to the air, squawking loudly. Red light rocketed from the ground near the trees which, together with the underbrush and soil, fell into a dark abyss. None of his puzzle preparation had helped at all today, but his continued emphasis on quick and careful movements did.

Adrien ignored the latest surge of destruction and continued to race forward. The red light vanished and left a patch of nothingness behind it, one of the many that now dotted the island. While the collapse started on the edges, they'd encountered several farther inland. Jackson had been injured by falling trees in an earlier close call.

"It's about a half-mile away," Adrien shouted. "That flare we saw looked farther back. If it's from the Krakens, we're closer than they are, but they're probably penned in as much as we are, so keep alert. Those Montreal players can be sneaky."

A roar rumbled ominously, and something thrashed through the jungle.

The captain muttered. A collapsing island was apparently not enough of a challenge. Dennis had to be subbed out after an earlier encounter with what might have been a cousin of whatever currently pursued them.

"Spread out," he ordered, stopped running, and turned toward the sound of splintering wood. They couldn't outrun the monster. He tightened his grip on his sword and layered another shield over himself. "Get ready. We'll use the same play as last time."

Carlos looked uneasy and the elf understood why. Dennis had nearly been eliminated when they tried the same strategy, although he wasn't sure if his fellow player was concerned about losing or had made the subtle mistake that many Louper players did of forgetting it was all a game and not real. When they were in the match, it was hard to tell.

"Just do it," he snapped.

His teammate nodded and jogged to hide behind a tree, as did the others. They all raised their wands and pointed them in the direction of the approaching threat.

It didn't take long. More trees dropped, and a huge shadow appeared in the distance. Adrien stood his ground. The features of a T-rex resolved into view a moment later. The dinosaur uttered another bone-shaking roar and charged.

Precious seconds passed as the beast moved closer. Its huge jaws, filled with sharp teeth, were intimidating even if the creature was fake. Louper was real enough that it was hard to not break and run, but the elf knew he needed to wait. He needed to trust in his team as they trusted in him. Dennis hadn't followed the plan. He'd tried to be a hero and had fallen victim to those massive jaws as a result. But, if everyone stuck to the plan, they could win.

Adrien drew a deep breath and aimed one hand at the ground. He began the incantation for a burst spell. The timing would need to be exquisite, but they could do this without losing any more players.

Four rainbow balls careened from behind the trees and directly toward the dinosaur to explode in showers of blinding sparks. The T-rex reared menacingly and uttered an echoing bellow of frustration. It was time.

The Light Elf released his spell and hurtled toward the blinded and agitated monster. He summoned another sword and raised both blades but took care not to shout or make any noise. His leap peaked, and he began to descend toward the animal. If the beast moved backward, the plan would probably end in his elimination when the colossus stamped his avatar out of existence.

The T-rex surged forward, and he grinned. He allowed himself a shout of triumph as his first blade pierced its eye smoothly. The dinosaur shook its head wildly in an effort to dislodge the blade, while the elf hung on his weapon. Adrien shouted a chant as he made careful movements with his free hand. A little transfiguration combined with a few tricks he'd learned would do the job.

He released his grip and fell. The shaking monster clipped him and catapulted him into a tree. He impacted abruptly with the trunk and thudded to sprawl awkwardly as he fought to regain his breath.

After a moment, he hissed through the pain and stood. His shields had, thankfully, absorbed the worst of the blow. He ducked behind a tree to reinforce his protection and finish his mental countdown from thirty.

The sword exploded in a shower of flame. As expected, the T-rex disappeared as the match officials valued challenge more than visual carnage.

"That worked way better than last time," Carlos shouted.

The captain ran in the direction of the pyramid. "It's all a matter of timing." To thrust a sword into a monster and then turn it into an explosive wasn't something he'd even think to try in a real fight, but it had worked for the moment. They couldn't bet on the Montreal Krakens having lost to every dinosaur they encountered.

The team continued to sprint for several more minutes and the pyramid gleamed even brighter as they approached through the trees. A violent tremor hurled them to their knees and several trees around them began to fall.

"Go, go, go," Adrien shouted. He burst forward.

Hilda, Irina, and Marcus whipped their wands down to copy their captain. Carlos hesitated, a mistake as he didn't clear the falling tree that crushed him.

The elf winced. Total player elimination meant no substitution. The red light appeared again, and the chunk of the island behind them vanished into the abyss.

The Cardinals continued, now only four strong. The next few tense minutes brought no more collapses or dinosaurs and they finally arrived at the bottom of the smooth golden pyramid. There seemed to be no easy way to climb without magical aid. A shout in the distance marked the appearance of the Krakens, three strong.

"Irina, you climb. Use a pinning spell, but wait for us to make our move," Adrien ordered. "Go steady rather than super-fast. The rest of you, come with me and make noise. We need to keep them focused on us." He sprinted a few feet before he released a burst spell. Halfway through his glide, he shouted a fireball incantation as loudly as possible.

The spell blasted toward the Kraken players in the distance. It exploded well away from them, but they scattered under the bombardment. Hilda and Marcus screamed their own spells, an ice blast and a thin electrical bolt, respectively. Again, neither shot came close.

Irina finished her spell and jogged up the side of the pyramid where she paused to take deep breaths, her wand pointed down. The pinning spell would stop her from sliding, but if she rushed too quickly, gravity might have its revenge.

The Kraken players opened fire with restraining spells, ropes, and chains. They flung these at the elf as he bounded toward them with burst spells. He dodged them, but he didn't make too much effort to remain under cover. Right now, the team was focused on him. He didn't even dare to look at Irina to check her progress and risk revealing the plan.

When he landed, he didn't deliver another attack. Instead, he concentrated and released a blinding spell. The Kraken all closed their eyes as the magic bathed their area in blinding white light. One member of the team even laughed, the harsh sound echoing in the distance.

"Nice try," the players shouted in the distance.

Another volley of restraining spells followed and this time, the ropes snagged and wrapped Adrien. He collapsed and landed hard on his back. Despite the awkwardness of his limited movement, he managed to roll hastily onto his side and turn his head toward Irina.

Three yards. Two yards. One yard.

He grinned.

The Kraken players finally caught on as she crested the pyramid. They yelled in disappointment.

The girl snatched the gleaming token and held it over her head. The captain might quibble with the execution of some of the team's tactics during the match, but he couldn't be mad about another victory. With this latest win and their continued perfect season, their place in the finals was all but assured.

CHAPTER NINE

Raine hummed quietly as she walked with Cameron down the narrow streets of Ruby Falls. She tried not to sigh. When he had suggested a low-key Valentine's Day, she hadn't objected. She spent every day with her boyfriend and he never let her down, so having him go over the top on a particular day didn't seem all that important. All that was true, but she also neglected to inform him of why she was so eager to go to the kemana and wander around.

They passed a dress shop, and some of her more duplicitous thoughts vanished to be replaced by fashion concerns. The Spring Formal lay ahead not all that far in the future, and she'd need to find something to wear.

Unfortunately, it was too early to purchase anything. The Student Council wasn't even sure if there would be a theme. It was a matter of intense debate from what she'd heard.

On some days, she missed being on Student Council. She'd needed to make sacrifices to fit FBI training time in with Agent Connor, and the council and horse riding were the two obvious activities she could eliminate. Someone might suggest that spending less time with her friends was a realistic choice, but they were one of the reasons she looked forward to coming to the school. It was hard to imagine the last few years without Sara, Evie, Philip, William, and Adrien, let alone Cameron. The people made the school.

Then again, not all her encounters there had been pleasant. Student Council had its share of annoying people, and her initial roommate situation hadn't been fun.

It didn't bother her. Bullies and cruel teenagers weren't new to her. In a sense, they were responsible for helping to awaken her magic back in Grand Rapids.

Another life—that's what it seemed like, even if the broad strokes remained the same. She would still become an FBI agent and follow in her father's footsteps, but everything important had changed. She was a magical, a witch, and had a shifter boyfriend. Not only that, but she would be the first openly serving magical in the FBI. Every experience, positive and negative, at the school was leading to that future.

Raine finally released a wistful sigh. She had promised herself she wouldn't let this last semester overwhelm her with melancholy. While she was ready to move on, that didn't mean it didn't hurt. That day, though, she wasn't in the kemana to worry too much about herself. Her real purpose was to look for suspicious people. Ruby Falls was filled with them, but she sought specific targets. She refocused on her original task.

A man with a scraggly beard walked down the street on

the opposite side and his gaze darted furtively at those around him. Raine followed his progress and stared at his hand. She wanted to see the back of his wrist and if he had any tattoos—in particular, the Eye of Thoth.

Cameron narrowed his eyes. "What's going on with you?"

There it was. Busted. It was only a matter of time.

She blinked and tried to look confused rather than guilty. "Huh? Going on with me?" She should have spent more time preparing her apology speech.

"Something's definitely going on." He nodded toward the man in the distance. "You're checking out a lot of people. It's like you're carefully examining everyone who looks remotely suspicious that we walk past, and no, that's not something you normally do." He sighed and folded his arms. "When I said, 'Let's enjoy each other's company' and you agreed so easily, you had an ulterior motive, didn't you? Here I was, patting myself on the back for how brilliant I was when the other guys stressed about the big day, but this isn't about simply spending time together."

"Um, no. I do want to spend time with you, but I thought I could multitask at the same time."

"Multitask?" The shifter smirked. "Okay, Miss Efficiency. What is included in this multitasking besides walking around with me?"

Raine rubbed the back of her neck. "I thought it wouldn't hurt while we were down here to look around in case we see some Thothites." She shrugged. "I'm not saying we have to confront them. We could get the police to deal with them, but an extra pair of eyes never hurts in a search.

And technically, everyone's looking for Cina and whatever other Thothites there might be hanging around."

Cameron shook his head and sighed. "I bet you'll be one of those people the bureau forces to go on vacation because you never take a day off and start to burn out. If you wanted to go look for Thothites, you could have simply said it. I wouldn't have said no."

"I'm sorry. It didn't sound very romantic to say, 'Hey, let's go look for cultists. Happy Valentine's Day.' But the PDA hasn't made any progress, and Madelyn's still locked up."

"She's not locked up. She's restricted to school grounds and she doesn't even seem to mind that much."

"Not much yet, if only because Erin can only sneak to the kemana. What about next year?" She frowned. "What if she's still stuck there next year and her friend can come and go as she pleases?"

"You don't know that'll happen," he said.

"It might, and I also know everyone's busy with stuff in the last semester, so I didn't want to ask them. But since you already said you wanted to go to the kemana, I thought it couldn't hurt." She shrugged.

"This is pointless."

She frowned. "Why do you say that? It's not pointless to try to protect our friend."

"I'm not saying that part is pointless." Cameron gestured around the area. "Think about it this way. Let's assume Cina is hanging around here, and that's a big assumption in and of itself."

Raine shook her head. "I don't agree. It's almost a certainty. Madelyn's critical to her plan. She definitely won't give up simply because she lost a few of her followers. And she doesn't have many options. She can blend in far easier in the kemana—even when using a disguise—than she can on the surface. It only makes sense that she's here. She can't exactly hide at the school, and if she even set foot inside, all the wards would have picked her up or Dorvu would have eaten her or something."

"Even if we buy into all those premises, you said it yourself. The PDA is here." He shrugged. "And even if it's only one agent at the school and one agent here, the Ruby Falls police are looking for Cina, too. That means even if she has stuck around or she has any lackeys left, there's no way we'll run into them walking down the street because she'll be careful and will keep a low profile. It's not realistic. I'm sorry, Raine. I know you want to help, but this isn't happening."

She sighed. "You're right, but I want to be sure. I feel like I'm not doing enough to help Madelyn."

"You already saved her and now, the federal government and local police are on the lookout. Unless you have something you can bring to the investigation they can't, I don't see the point in worrying about it." Cameron placed a hand on her shoulder and gave it a comforting squeeze. "We've done so much these last few years, and we've helped many people, but we also have to accept that sometimes, we've been lucky and sometimes, we've had help. It wasn't always only the FBI Trouble Squad running off to save the day."

"I know all that, Cameron." Raine shook her head. "I'm simply afraid I'll graduate and Madelyn will still be forced to stay on campus. It's not fair, and I feel like I'll be letting her and Vianna down if I leave before Cina's taken care of."

"If—and only if—we had some kind of clue that would lead us to Cina, I'd back you. I wouldn't be happy about it, but I know how stubborn you are and I know you'd do it anyway, so I'd be forced to help you." He gestured around the street filled with dress and accessory shops, along with the occasional cart. "But we have no clue. We have no leads." He pointed to a bright green wooden flower cart manned by a dour dwarf. "But we do have flowers, and it's Valentine's Day. I want you to shut your brain down, *Agent* Campbell, and enjoy the day. For now, Madelyn's safe, and like I said, she's not even all that worried about being stuck on campus."

She took a deep breath and released it slowly. "Okay, fair enough. I'll try to concentrate on spending time with you and not worrying about the Thothites."

"There you go. It's not so hard, is it?" He smiled. "Happy Valentine's Day." He bowed. "My gift to you, fair lady, is the gift of distraction."

She laughed. "I accept your gift."

CHAPTER TEN

An hour into a painting session in the Art Room, an idea crept into Sara's mind. It seemed obvious in retrospect, but most great ideas did. She set her brushes down and removed her apron before she hurried over to Madelyn's room in hopes of catching the girl there to discuss the possibility.

As she walked, she realized she would miss how close everything was at the School of Necessary Magic. Her college situation wouldn't be as convenient, even though she would have some magical instructors. She doubted the cafeteria would involve pixies and custom meals appearing before her.

A small chuckle escaped her, and a passing boy gave her an odd look.

"I thought about a funny joke I heard earlier," she said as a hasty explanation.

He shrugged and continued without another glance.

If she had not gone to the school, would her magic have come in all the way? Her family seemed obsessed with the idea that it would either happen or not, but the challenges she faced along with her friends were hard to dismiss. Maybe it was more like a muscle that needed exercise.

Sara whistled as she proceeded down the hallway toward Madelyn's room. She knocked and bounced a little on the balls of her feet, and her heart pounded. Inspiration was always exhilarating, but she didn't want to get too far ahead of herself. Her plan required Madelyn's agreement, and even if the girl had grown less shy, that didn't mean she was always comfortable around people who randomly showed up to talk to her. Besides that, there was no guarantee she would even like the suggestion.

There was even a small chance it might offend her, but she had to take the risk. It wasn't for her sake. The art involved wouldn't be groundbreaking or challenge her technique, but she was certain it would help Madelyn.

The door opened to reveal the Coral Elf. She cocked her head and uncertainty played across her face. "Sara?"

"That's me last time I checked."

"Is something wrong?"

The kitsune shook her head. "Why would you ask that?"

Madelyn sighed. "It's only that you never talk to me unless Raine's around. I wasn't sure you liked me."

"No, no. I like you. It's just... I don't know. It's weird at this point. Here's me talking to you now, though, right?" She shrugged.

"I suppose so. What do you need?"

"Are you busy? There's something I wanted to talk to you about. An art project. Nothing big, only a little idea I wanted to bounce off you. I think you'll find it interesting, but I didn't want to start it before I had your explicit permission."

The girl shrugged and gestured for her to enter. "I was reading about the contribution of secret Carthaginian magical forces to the Battle of Cannae. It's interesting to me how much magic has influenced history when it was supposed to not be used much. I understand that they kept it secret, but I wonder if they hadn't used it if it wouldn't have ended with Roman-allied wizards using their own magic in later battles."

Sara entered the room and closed the door behind her. "I think it was harder to control things back in the day. They didn't have the kind of enforcement more organized groups like the Silver Griffins brought. And those ancient wizards hid it well enough. It's not like normal history books up to twenty years ago mentioned any suspicious magic for most of these things." She smiled. "Anyway, I'm not here to talk about military history. To be honest, I don't know much about it at all, and I only know about that battle because Cameron mentioned it once. But I do have something else I wanted to run by you. Like I said, an art project—specifically, a painting project."

Madelyn nodded slowly and a hint of panic crept onto her face. "O-okay. What art project?"

The kitsune waved her hands in front of her in an attempt to appear non-threatening. "It's nothing dangerous or complicated or spooky. I'm working on portraits right now in Art Club, and I thought about doing a portrait of you and another one of your sister. I can use pictures, so you don't have to sit around and pose for me. Like I said, nothing dangerous or too involved. But I didn't want to do a painting of you, let alone one of your sister, without you being okay with it. It's not that I think it'll have any magical effects or anything, but I do understand how difficult it has been for you to adjust to living here."

Her companion stared at her in silence and for a long moment, she didn't even blink. She didn't look mad, confused, annoyed, or happy. In fact, she didn't look like she felt much of anything. Sara had no idea how to interpret that, so she forged ahead with her explanation. Maybe the girl needed more details.

"I also thought of using magic with the portraits, too. I'll admit that is something I need more practice on." She shrugged. "It won't be anything major. I'll simply add a little motion. Many people, even magicals, like paintings with a little motion. Not too much—it won't be a movie or anything, merely a little nicer. It's easier, you see, to have a painting like that than to cast an illusion spell. It takes me longer to produce, but it's far more permanent."

Madelyn continued to stare and the corners of her mouth twitched.

Sara forced a smile and wondered if she'd offended the girl with her suggestion of painting Vianna. She had hoped it could serve as a memorial piece. The Coral Elf spoke often enough of her sister that it was obvious she still needed time to come to terms with her death. Her art was one of the few things she could offer the suffering girl, but she'd obviously miscalculated—and, judging by the reaction, badly.

"I'm sorry," she murmured and sighed. "I didn't think it through. I thought you would like the idea, but if you don't, it's fine. I can find other subjects. It's not like I'm locked into doing it. I simply thought of it when I was painting an—"

The girl threw her arms around Sara. The kitsune froze, her brain not sure for a second if she was being attacked or hugged. It wasn't like she could knock Madelyn out without angering Headmistress Berens and Raine. Fortunately, the arm movement was a prelude to a comfortable squeeze and not a brutal tackle.

The Coral Elf looked up and tears trickled down her cheeks. "Thank you so much, Sara. I-I don't care so much about a painting of me, but that's nice, too. But the idea of a painting of Vianna—the fact that you even thought to do one makes me feel like she's still alive. I'll treasure this painting for the rest of my life, I promise you. And I've seen your art, so I know you'll do a good job."

"Okay, then." Sara blinked, still not quite caught up with the shift in mood. She grinned a few seconds later. "It looks like I have my next two painting projects."

"Now that I think about, I have only one request."

"Sure. What is it?"

"I don't want separate paintings. I want a painting of me with Vianna." Madelyn pulled away from her and wiped her tears. "It'll mean more to me that way. It'll be like the one last thing we'll do together."

She nodded. "Sure thing. I can do that. Any other requests?"

The elf shook her head. "No. I'm just happy you're doing that."

"I'm happy to do it, and it's the least I can do for a friend. I don't think I've ever run into someone so happy for me to do a painting before." She rubbed her hands together. "I'll grab some photos from you and get started. Now, I'm really fired up."

As Madelyn turned to open her desk, Sara pumped her fist. This was what art meant, and it was important that she remind herself of that. Art wasn't merely pretty objects made to entertain. It was about touching the soul. She didn't have to be an FBI agent or work at a charity to help people.

CHAPTER ELEVEN

Raine leaned back against the couch and nibbled her lip. The latest movie night film, *Signs,* was over and now in its credits. In their last session, they had watched *Unbreakable*. That had resulted in a split opinion with Adrien, Cameron, Raine, and William liking it, but Sara, Evie, Madelyn, and Philip not liking it. The superhero-themed film did invoke another discussion of the responsibility that came with power.

"Huh." Philip frowned a little as the credits continued to scroll. "That movie wasn't as twisty as *Unbreakable* or *The Sixth Sense*."

William shrugged. "Maybe he tried to get away from that."

"You don't think it had a twist?" Sara pursed her lips and shook her head. "The way they won was kind of a twist, especially since all the signs throughout the movie pointed toward what was going to happen."

Adrien scoffed. "I don't understand how the aliens could have that particular weakness given that they were attacking Earth. It's like attacking France and being weak against quality cuisine."

Raine laughed and shook her head. "Now that's an interesting metaphor, but I don't know if they're supposed to be aliens. I mean, like alien-aliens as opposed to demons."

"Demons?" The Light Elf frowned. "Where did you get that idea? I thought it was rather clear they were extraterrestrials with no mystical powers."

"There are a lot of religious themes in the film, after all. It's about losing and recovering faith, and they talk about the counterattack method being first discovered in the Middle East, which links in with religion given it's the birthplace of several major Earth religions. Maybe what they used was blessed somehow." She shrugged. "Although sometimes, invading forces simply do dumb stuff or they're desperate. Who knows? The entire invasion might have been dumb kids."

"Like in *Explorers*," Philip said. "Sure, maybe." He shook his finger at the TV. "Every time I watch anything about aliens, it makes me wonder. Everyone used to tell stories about faeries and monsters in the forests kidnapping people and weird lights and stuff, and then they all went away, and people started saying it was aliens."

"What are you getting at?" She asked.

"We're all taught that all that alien stuff is misinterpretation, right?" He swept the room with his wide-eyed gaze. "That all real alien encounters were only with Oricerans. But nothing we've learned about magic suggests the rest of the universe doesn't exist. Those are real stars out there with real planets."

Cameron frowned. "Nobody said they weren't."

Philip nodded. "It's the Fermi Paradox, dude. It looks like the universe should be filled with intelligent life, and for the longest time, people couldn't find any other than humans, so people spent a lot of time trying to find out why. At least people who didn't know about magic."

Raine gestured toward Adrien. "But everyone knows about other intelligent species. There are thousands on Oriceran, let alone all the ones we have living on Earth now. There is no Fermi Paradox."

The wizard grinned. "Exactly!"

Sara scooted away from him. "Don't go crazy on me yet."

"Don't you get it?" He pointed at Adrien and then Madelyn, who blinked. "Let's set aside all the witches and wizards in this room. We have a Light Elf who can trace his heritage to another planet, and a Coral Elf who is even more special, but that only makes the Fermi Paradox worse."

"I don't understand," Raine said. "Why would it make it worse rather than resolve it?"

"Because the fact that we know there are thousands of intelligent species means intelligent life isn't super-rare and that it can arise in a number of different ways. But everyone still says, 'Nope, the only aliens are people from Oriceran. There are no aliens from outer space.' And Oriceran might not technically even be in our universe, and if it is, it's so far away that it might as well not be. There are places like the World in Between and some of these other dimensions that can even be messed with given the appropriate magic." Philip hopped up and rubbed his chin. "Don't you see, though? Why did we give up on outer space aliens? Everyone seems convinced that it's silly to believe in them, but it makes more sense to believe in them than the opposite. Maybe they're still out there. I'm not saying they've visited, though. I don't believe that." He scoffed.

"Why?" she asked.

"They might be able to hide from technology, but how can they hide from magic?" Philip shrugged as if were the most obvious thing in the world.

Madelyn finished swallowing a handful of M&Ms. Small chocolate stains decorated her pale cheeks. "Why can't they be magical, too?"

"Huh?" He turned to face her.

"The aliens. You seem to assume it's only Earth and Oriceran that are magical. Why can't every planet be magical?"

He frowned. "Well, Earth lacks decent magical energy without the gates to Oriceran being open. So isn't Oriceran the center of all magic?"

"We don't know enough to say that," Adrien said. "There might be some other alien planet paired with another magical world, or maybe Earth is the only planet that needs another planet to feed its magic. Perhaps the space aliens aren't coming to Earth because the magical situation here is so primitive and they've waited for the planet to mature magically. Perhaps they'll come in a few centuries."

"Why haven't they come to Oriceran, then?" Cameron asked.

Raine nodded her agreement with that question.

"I don't know," the elf responded. "Maybe they can't reach it. I do feel that Madelyn has a point. We can't assume anything about other planets in this galaxy, let alone the universe. They might be loaded with intelligent magical beings who don't have any advanced technological infrastructure or any links to other planets because they have no need of such things. If they have no reason to leave their planet and their resources are well-maintained with the help of magic, we might not ever see them."

The Coral Elf set her M&M bowl down. "Maybe they have come and we simply don't know about it."

Philip sighed. "I can't bring myself to believe that. Even if they had magic, it'd be hard to hide."

"I spent a lot of time during the break reading about magical history and all the groups who covered up the existence of magic, including the various governments." She blew out a breath. "I-I don't know if it's true, but it's not impossible that the governments might be hiding the existence of non-Oriceran extraterrestrials on purpose. It'd be even easier because they can freely use magic to do it."

"But why?" Raine asked. "I don't know if I agree with Philip that they would be unable to hide necessarily, but everyone knows about Oriceran. Elves, gnomes, and dwarves walk the streets. In some of the bigger cities, you see very strange races that humans can't even relate to. There wouldn't be a big panic if the government admitted that aliens were real. I think most people would be like Philip and say, 'I always believed that was the case.'"

Cameron snapped his fingers. "I have a theory. Not that I think aliens are real, of course. That's silly."

"Silly like being a werewolf?" Raine asked. She poked him in the shoulder.

"Yes. Unlike aliens, I'm real." He gave her a toothy grin.

"What's your big theory, dude?" Philip asked.

"Fear," the shifter said. "Raine's wrong because she's forgetting military differentials."

"Military differentials?" She frowned at him. "Why would there be military differentials?"

"Even if they don't have magic, they might have hyper-advanced weapons. If the governments of Earth and Oriceran can't reliably say they can defend the planet from aliens, there's no point in even admitting they exist. People might panic, exactly like everyone did in the old days. At least with Oriceran, there were Earth magicals as well." He shrugged. "For all we know, there could be whole alliances of advanced races with technology centuries beyond this planet and magic centuries beyond what we know. Maybe they've combined it and can drop curse bombs that wipe out entire continents."

Evie sighed. "Why would they have to be evil simply because they're more advanced?"

"They don't have to, but it's hard for an advanced race not to harm a less advanced race." Cameron snorted. "Especially if they have something they want."

"Maybe it'll be like *Signs*," William said. He shrugged when everyone turned to look at him. "The aliens were obviously way more advanced than normal humans, but in the end, they had a weakness that was easy to exploit. It could be that some big advanced aliens show up with a fleet of spaceships, but they don't have the most basic defenses against magic. In that case, they might not come because they're afraid of us."

Philip clapped once. "I had the coolest idea."

"About aliens?"

He shook his head. "Remember that time we watched *Independence Day*—I can't remember if it was last semester or the semester before that, but we spent all that time discussing the virus."

Everyone nodded.

"That was a pre-gate movie." He grinned. "They should totally remake it but set it before the gates open and have the humans win because a group of wizards come out of hiding and use magic on the aliens. A remake for the modern age. Shyamalan can do it. It can be a twist. Like it comes out of nowhere in the last ten minutes."

"I don't think a good twist comes out of nowhere," Raine said.

"Yeah." Sara nodded. "I liked *Signs* better than *Unbreakable*, and I liked *The Sixth Sense* better than both of them, but one thing I'll say is the twists all have clues pointing to them. They don't technically come out of nowhere. Like in *Signs*, everything from his wife's dying words to the little girl's habit all point to the twist, if you're going to call it that, and it's even stronger in the other two movies."

Philip nodded. "I can see what you mean. I wonder if we'll get tired of twists. I know not all his films have them, but it is kind of his thing."

"I don't care if it has a twist," Raine said. "I only care if it's a good movie."

CHAPTER TWELVE

Sara waved to Raine as they stepped out of potions class. She sniffed her blazer. "Huh. Professor Fowler was right. The smell didn't last long."

Raine laughed. "Not that smelling it for a few minutes wasn't bad enough. I don't know how Evie can handle some of that." She glanced inside the room. Their friend was still chatting with Professor Fowler and told them she would catch up with them.

The kitsune slung her backpack over her shoulder. "Not to pull an Evie, but you go ahead. I'm not that hungry, and I wanted to check on something in the art room while I think of it. By the time I get there and do everything, lunch will be halfway over."

"Are you sure?"

She nodded. "It's no big deal."

"Okay, see you soon," Raine replied with a smile. "Don't skip dinner."

Sara waved and continued down the hallway. Students formed flowing streams both ways, a current she'd gotten used to over the years. Would it feel the same way at college, or would it be impersonal? The School of Necessary Magic had become home, familiar and safe, but everyone had to leave home eventually.

She turned a corner still thinking about college. Jillian, an all too familiar gray-haired elf girl, all but jumped from the wall in front of her. The Gray Elf, among other things, was the current leader of the Live Unnecessary Tricksters. The implications and timing of her appearance weren't lost on Sara.

"What?" she asked and tried to keep the irritation out of her voice.

Jillian looked cautiously around her before she leaned in to whisper, "It's coming. It's only weeks away. We need you."

Sara groaned. It was exactly what she feared. "April Fool's Day."

"Exactly." The elf tilted her chin and a look of smug certainty spread over her face. "We want you to participate in the prank war. No, we need you. We need the unpredictability that only a kitsune can bring."

"Are you insane?" She backed away and shook her head. "Don't you remember what happened last year? You were almost killed, and I appreciate that you saved Raine, but she could have been killed, too."

"And I apologized for Raine getting involved, but I've had a year to think about it. That whole situation wasn't fair, and it's not reflective of a Trickster event. The magic of Eris tampered with everything. It's not as if pranks, magical or not, are inherently dangerous, and I refuse to let the corruption of that witch destroy what our society has built up. I paid for what happened when I protected Raine."

Sara sighed and shook her head. "I can't believe I'm hearing this. I honestly have no idea how to even respond to it. I know you were still doing a few pranks here and there after what happened, but I assumed that once you left for the summer, you would come back not as interested."

"Everything great requires risk to accomplish." Jillian sniffed disdainfully. "And although I wasn't happy that Raine was exposed to risk because of how Eris tampered with things, that doesn't change the fact that pranks rarely threaten lives, whereas your little Trouble Squad often purposefully exposes themselves to danger. The prank last year was the only one I've ever been involved in where I or anyone I know was hurt, but you all are under threat every semester from what I've heard."

The kitsune snorted. "We do that to save and help people, not simply because we're bored and have something to prove." She shook her head. "Don't you get it? I understand that the prank war won't be as dangerous because there's no chaos witch to mess things up, but I don't know what to say. I still can't look at a cupcake because of some spell misfiring when I first got here. What can I say? I'm an artist. My soul bruises easily, and I can't bring myself to be involved, not simply for jokes and not after you were hurt and my best friend was almost killed."

"They aren't simply jokes," the Gray Elf thundered and earned the stares and confused looks of a few other students down the hallway. She lowered her voice. "They are so much more than that."

"I don't understand." Sara blinked. The other girl was normally so cool and collected, if not condescending.

Jillian looked down. "You don't understand what it's like. I'm a Gray Elf. We can see the future, even if not all the time. Do you have any idea what that does to you when you think about it too much? If I see the future and I change my actions, was it the future? If I don't, am I actually making a choice? It's bothered me for as long as I can remember. It's one of the reasons my people are so into order and going after those who might disrupt it." She squeezed her hands into fists and took a deep breath. "That's why I use the artifact to suppress my powers much of the time and look forward to the prank wars. Pranks surprise sometimes, but often they don't. They're not simply jokes. They are living experiments that prove the universe and existence is more than a mindless machine awaiting input to give the exact output. They teach the paradox of both control and a lack of control. They're almost more important to me than my magic."

Sara didn't respond for a long time as she locked eyes with her companion. The few students who lingered nearby wandered off, now uninterested in the rapidly defusing situation. Reasonable conversations were boring.

"I didn't…" She sighed and looked away. "I thought it was about competition and being better than other people for you. I never realized you had thought so deeply about them or that they meant so much to you. It's almost like pranks, to you, are as important as my painting is to me."

Jillian nodded. "Yes. I'm not like you, Sara. My soul doesn't bruise so easily. I'm not saying this makes me better or worse than you, merely different. I know everyone finds me cold and aloof most of the time, and I doubt I could produce the kind of art you do, but pranks bring me joy and not only the joy of defeating an opponent."

"Fair enough." The kitsune smiled. "I appreciate where you're coming from now, but I still can't participate. I don't want to be involved anymore. Every time I think about pranks, I think about how close you and Raine came to getting killed. To me, they were about fun, and they aren't fun for me anymore. They're something that stresses me out."

"I can respect that." The girl sighed. "The difficult path of a Trickster isn't for everyone, even a kitsune, but I thought I'd try. That doesn't mean the rest of us won't engage in the prank war." She turned and offered a quick wave. "You can't blame me for asking. After all, I was the one who was hurt the most."

"I know, and I understand that it all comes down to being Eris' fault in the end. Good luck, Jillian. I hope you give the rest of the Tricksters a hard time."

The elf looked over her shoulder with a thin smile. "Thank you. I will."

Sara waved as the girl wandered down the hallway. She wanted to believe it was over, but even if Jillian accepted her explanation, would the other Tricksters be so willing to leave the kitsune out of it?

CHAPTER THIRTEEN

Raine strolled down the hall on her way to visit Madelyn. She hadn't talked to the other girl for a few days, and she wanted to check in on her. They only talked at length during movie nights, and those were more a weekend affair. Although she'd seemed okay during their last conversation, people's attitudes could change quickly.

If anyone had asked, she would have admitted she was more worried than Madelyn about Cina and being stuck at the School of Necessary Magic. No matter how much sense it made for the girl's safety, the unfairness of the entire situation continued to prick at Raine's mind. Her forays into the kemana hadn't netted anything but dress ideas and good meals. Cameron had been right. If the Thothites were still present, they did a good job of hiding.

That didn't matter. Raine would continue to do her best to support Madelyn in any way she could. Wasting a few hours in the kemana or chatting with a friend weren't exactly the greatest hardships on the planet.

She turned a corner and slowed as she approached the room.

The Coral Elf stood near the open door to her room, her hand on her roommate Erin's arm and her eyes wide in panic. "Y-you shouldn't be going."

"You said that already," Erin said with a frown. "And I keep telling you it's not a big deal. Don't you want me to have some fun with the others?"

"Yes, b-but...can't they do something at the school? Like I said, it's not safe."

The other girl shook Madelyn's hand off and frowned. "Thanks, *Mom*," she said and rolled her eyes. "I'm tired of talking about this. I'm going to the library now, but I'll be back later. Maybe you can remember what it's like to be reasonable by then." She stormed away, red-faced. She almost slammed into Raine, barely stepped around her at the last second, and made no effort to offer any apology.

Raine blinked and looked at Madelyn, whose eyes were glistening, then at Erin. She shrugged and hurried toward the elf. "Are you okay?"

She gestured inside her room. "I-I don't want to talk in the hallway."

They entered quickly and Madelyn closed the door. She took a few steps toward her desk before she burst into tears.

"Whoa," Raine said. "Calm down. I'm here. We can talk about whatever just happened. I'm sure I can help."

The girl sobbed for several more seconds before she managed to bring it down to a sniffle. She wiped her face with her sleeve. "It's all over."

"What's all over?" Raine nodded toward the door. "Is something wrong with Erin?"

"She hates me now. She'll probably ask the headmistress to move out. I'm sure she regrets ever moving in."

She sighed. "What were you arguing about? Did you have some sort of disagreement about the room?"

Madelyn dropped into a chair behind her desk. She shook her head before she laid it on her desk, her long blue hair concealing much of her face except her differently colored eyes. "No. Erin always says I'm easy to live with because I don't have a strong opinion about anything in the room," she murmured, her voice barely above a whisper.

"Then what's the problem?"

"The kemana."

"The kemana? What about it?"

"Erin was invited to visit there with some other friends of hers. She hasn't gone there before because it's against the rules."

Raine nodded. She often forgot that Madelyn's roommate was only a freshman. It wasn't common to room different grade levels, but Christie had been with them until the previous year, so it wasn't like the other girl's situation was unique.

Madelyn sighed. "I told Erin she shouldn't go to the kemana with other freshmen because it's unsafe, and she said I worry too much. She said I let my own experiences prejudice things." She groaned. "But there are bad people there who aren't Cina and her people."

"Ruby Falls can be dangerous, and there can be bad people there, but it's really only a town like any other. Well, a magical town like any other, and it's almost a Rite of

Passage for freshmen to go there, even against the rules. I'm surprised Erin hasn't done it earlier."

"She's afraid of a lot of stuff." The elf shrugged. "She's an introvert, too. It's why we get along. I think she only feels brave because five of her other friends are going. She doesn't hang out with them much, but they've tried to get her to go to the kemana for a long time."

Raine shrugged. "It's not a big deal. I went to the kemana in the first semester." Mentioning her involvement in the druid case would only reinforce the safety issue, so she decided against it.

"But you're not like Erin. She's not brave and strong like you." Madelyn lifted her head and let it loll back. "And I know I went to the kemana with Vianna as freshmen, but we didn't do it to have fun, and I had Vianna to help protect me even if I was still a coward." She sighed. "I still am, but now at least I have stuff to fight for."

"I get why you're concerned, but the basic reality is that ninety-nine percent of students go into the kemana without any trouble at all." She folded her arms and leaned against the door. "My trouble and your problems are the exceptions. We're both special in an annoying way." She shrugged. "And even in my case, almost every time I've gone into the kemana, I haven't had any serious trouble. And as I'm sure Cameron will tell you, if I minded my own business, I wouldn't have had a lot of that trouble."

"I didn't want to make her mad. I only wanted to protect her, and now, I've screwed everything up." Madelyn straightened and shook her head. "I just…" She groaned.

"You just what?"

She frowned. "I would feel better if I could go with her to protect her. I know that sounds silly because I can barely protect myself at times, but m-my magic is stronger in many ways than most other sophomores."

Raine smiled. "You sound like Cameron with me. There's nothing wrong with wanting to protect the people you care about. Most people would consider that a good thing."

The girl faced her. "But I can't go into the kemana and not only because of the rules. It might not be that dangerous for Erin, but it's far too dangerous for me."

"I agree. Cina's strong. Even one of the professors would have trouble facing her by themselves, and you should stay well away from the kemana until the PDA captures and locks her up. I don't know if she's still around, but if you leave this place, she might be able to grab you and use one of her portal beads. It's not fair, and it makes me angry simply thinking about it, but that's the way it is."

"I know, and I agree." Madelyn rested her head on the desk again. "But now. Erin will hate me. She likes me and we do things together, but I made her mad and now, she'll leave me."

"It's not like that." Raine lowered her arms and sighed. "Let me put it to you this way. I know you were frustrated with how overprotective Vianna could be, but did you hate her?"

The elf shook her head. "Of course not. She was trying to help me. While she wasn't always right, I knew it wasn't coming from a bad place. But that's not the same thing."

"Why is that?"

"Because she was my sister, my other half."

She nodded. "Okay, but it's really not all that different. I know you're still learning about this, but you have to understand that friendship isn't always thoughtful movie nights and fun conversations."

"What do you mean?"

"It's a lot like with Vianna." Raine shrugged. "People are…people. We all have our opinions, thoughts, and feelings. Sometimes, that means we fight. I've gotten in fights with my friends. I've gotten in huge fights with my boyfriend. Having a close relationship with someone doesn't mean you'll never get in a fight. It simply means you'll have to make up afterward."

"Really?" Madelyn's voice wavered. "Are you sure she doesn't hate me?"

"I think that if the worst thing you've done is make Erin think you're overprotective, you won't have a problem at all making up with her. Part of friendship is disagreeing, and I don't know any good friends who haven't had at least one disagreement. She doesn't hate you. You can talk it out later, and I'm sure it won't be a big deal."

The elf took a deep breath and exhaled slowly. Her cheeks remained puffy and red, but her eyes were dry. "O-okay. I'll try talking to her later. Thanks, Raine."

"No problem. I'm glad I could be of help."

CHAPTER FOURTEEN

Raine smiled at dinner as she bit into her roasted chicken leg. The absolutely perfect seasoning wasn't surprising. No matter how much a few of the pixies denied it, she always assumed they used a dash of magic to ensure the quality of their meals.

Cameron grinned at her. "It's that good? You've smiled for the last minute."

She shook her head and nodded toward the other side of the room. Madelyn sat with Erin, smiling and chatting with her friend. They'd been there for several minutes and their camaraderie lightened her mood.

He glanced at the two girls. "What about them?"

She set her chicken back on her plate. "Madelyn got in a fight with Erin earlier, and she was worried they would never make up. I've wondered if it's a bad thing that she doesn't eat with us, but I realize now it's a good thing."

"It'd be too weird for her friend to sit around with a bunch of seniors." He shrugged. "She needs to have friends who won't immediately leave, and it might even help to have friends who are more…normal."

"How are we not normal?" She frowned.

"Name another group of friends in this school who have been as involved in as much trouble as we have. The one semester we didn't stumble on some seriously messed up stuff still involved…" He glanced around and leaned closer to her. "It still involved a secret magical society," he whispered.

"Okay, I'll grant you that. We're an unusual group."

"That's why we're the FBI Trouble Squad, right?" Philip interjected with a grin. "At least we're not boring."

"Even ignoring all that, Madelyn needs to learn to solve her own problems," Sara said after a sip of her iced water. She eyed Raine with suspicion. "I'm not saying you never have to offer any big sisterly advice, and I'm helping her out too in my own way. The problem is that her personality is such that she's looking for a sister-type to tell her what to do, and that means she might not think for herself when she needs to." She sighed. "You didn't get involved, did you?"

Philip and William snickered. Evie looked concerned. Adrien wasn't there to offer his opinion. He'd grabbed a quick bite to eat before he rushed off to another Louper practice.

The large number of hours the team put into practice was amazing, but their record spoke for itself. Not only had they maintained a perfect season, but their last couple of matches hadn't even been close. It wasn't an exaggeration to say the Cardinals currently dominated their competition.

Raine laughed. "No, I didn't get involved. Well, I kind of did." She waved her hands defensively in front of her. "I went to talk to Madelyn earlier, but it wasn't about anything like that. I only wanted to chat with her. She eats with Erin all the time now rather than us, so I really only see her in passing in the library on occasion or movie nights. I worry about her. I'm happy she has a friend like Erin, but I also understand the kind of thing she went through better than most people."

Cameron stared at her. "You're not jealous, are you?"

"No, I'm not jealous. I'm the same as I've always been—a worried busybody." She shrugged.

Everyone laughed.

Sara grinned. "You'll soon be able to channel your passion for being a worried busybody into a career." She gave her a thumbs-up. "Go you."

"Being an FBI agent won't make me a busybody. It only means I'll be law enforcement."

"Same difference." Her friend winked.

Evie finished with her final spoonful of a color-changing gelatin dessert, a special treat from Tori. She hadn't been able to spend as much time with the pixies that semester due to her commitments to Professor Fowler.

She smiled. "It's not too late if any of you want to get involved in the extra-curricular potion projects. Does anyone want in? It's not only useful if you're going into potions like me. There are a lot of advanced practical skills covered that she can't get into in class for various reasons. I'm sure you could find something useful."

William shook his head. "Sorry. I'm still too busy with FBI training. Even if I don't go right away, I will do some internship work with the bureau during college. Every scrap of information I learn about FBI technique and criminal history will help me get the most out of the internship. I still feel like I'm way behind Raine, to be honest."

"I don't think that, and I know Agent Connor doesn't think that, either." Raine sighed. "And you're sure about not going in directly?"

He nodded. "Yes, and Agent Connor understands that." He smiled. "I'm not saying you're wrong to join right away, Raine, but I'm not you. I didn't come from an FBI family. You've talked about looking into case histories from when you were a kid. I still feel like I need time to get into the mindset. That's what I mean about being behind."

"I suppose it's not like even if you joined right away that we would work closely together. Maybe I'm being selfish."

"Forget the FBI." Cameron grinned. "Is there no chance of you trying to join the Secret Service with me, William?"

Raine frowned. "Don't poach my fellow agent. The next thing we know, Adrien will show up and ask everyone to become a Guardian."

"Take your time and enjoy life, dude," Philip said. "You don't need to be deep into your career before you're even twenty-one." He looked at Evie and then Raine. "Not that it's a bad thing, necessarily."

Evie shook her head. "I might not go to formal college, but I'll be an apprentice for years, so only Raine will get years of experience before she's twenty-one."

"Being in the FBI was always my future in one way or another," Raine said. "Although being a magical changes things because it's helped me get in sooner." She surveyed the dining hall and all the students there. "Everything's changing. Magicals will be everywhere in a few decades. I think people will look back and wonder why the heck they weren't allowed to serve in agencies like the FBI before. Maybe they won't even need special AET teams for the police because there will be enough magicals in the police departments."

"Maybe." A solemn look descended over Cameron. "But there will always be more non-magicals on Earth than magicals, right?"

Philip frowned as he thought about that. "Are we sure? Last time the gates were open, they didn't have advanced science. One thing I've learned in the Entrepreneurs' Club is that there's considerable opportunity for technology and magic to mix, and that's not even counting things like genetics."

Sara looked at him with a blank expression. "Genetics?"

The wizard nodded. "We know that magical ability is partially inherited, and genetic engineering is improving every year even without magic. Just saying. Think about the implications."

Raine made a face. "I don't necessarily like the idea of people messing with people's genes to give them magic. What if there are some side-effects they don't know about?"

Cameron nodded. "Messing around with people to change them for the future reminds me a little too much of what the dark wizards did with shifters."

Philip groaned. "You're making it sound so creepy. For all we know, it'll happen naturally, and even if they don't genetically engineer people, technomagic will still be a thing. You know what? It's already a thing. You should see some of the things being brought to market soon."

She shrugged. "I don't really care much about technology. Fancy gadgets don't help much with potions."

The wizard rubbed his temples in disbelief. "The point is that Carlyle brings technomagic gadgets to the masses in a big way. In five years, I wouldn't be surprised if AMS is the single largest company in the world. I bet you in say, three years, everyone will be talking about Scott Carlyle all the time and saying how he's almost saving the world. He'll change the world for the better. He'll bring magicals and non-magicals together through the power of technology, and he's talked about that being one of his big goals. I almost thought about trying to work for him, but I'm more interested in non-profit work."

Raine nodded. "I've read a little about him. Law enforcement is very interested in many technomagic inventions. Several companies are working on anti-magic devices to help apprehend and contain magical criminals."

She nodded. "I think that will help. If Cameron's right and there are always more non-magicals than magicals on Earth, the authorities need ways to take care of criminals that don't rely on bounty hunters." She made a face. As far as she was concerned, bounty hunters were one step up from criminals. The police and federal law enforcement should handle problems, not gun-toting glorified vigilantes.

Philip smiled. "It sounds like we're graduating at the right time. There are so many opportunities and a chance to make a real difference."

"You're right," Sara said. "If I'd joined my art program

right after the gates opened, people might still be afraid of me. But now they're used to it, so they can focus on my art instead of the fact I'm a magical."

"I can't say things will be that different for me as a potions witch," Evie said. "But it might be nice if more people were comfortable with potions in general. It means they can be better integrated into daily life, and maybe more people would take an interest in sourcing ingredients so they don't end up so expensive."

"This is great," Raine said. "We'll all go our separate ways but at the right time to really help the world." She looked at the smiling Madelyn. Head Librarian Decker insisted that it was arrogant to think a person lived in a special time, but maybe it didn't matter if the era was unique, as long as that same person always tried to make the world a better place.

After all, the FBI Trouble Squad had made the School of Necessary Magic a better place in their own way.

CHAPTER FIFTEEN

Adrien grinned as the mast of one of the old galleons cracked and pitched forward. It smashed into the deck to launch wood and nails like shrapnel. In addition, it clipped two Orono players, including Finn. They grunted as they fell into the ocean.

The fins of dozens of sharks cut through the water as the underwater Louper obstacles rushed toward the downed players. A few double fins from other mysterious seas creatures joined them. Falling in the water wasn't advised for anyone who wanted to avoid elimination.

He gestured to the next ship. "Let's move. We're so close but won't win the quarter-finals by sitting around."

The entire Cardinals line-up burst across to the next galleon. Dennis, Carlos, Marcus, Hilda, and Jackson were all still in play and they hadn't had to substitute anyone yet.

The current Louper match involved the simulated high seas and a fleet of hundreds of different old Spanish galleons, their white sails fluttering in the wind. The vessels bobbed in the water but never moved nearer or farther from one another.

Each flew different flags with a series of unique dots, obviously some kind of code. Adrien suspected that even if they hadn't found the map, the dots provided a second chance. They hadn't paid much attention to them since they knew exactly where they were going. Running into the Orono Ouroboros only confirmed they were on the right path.

After another couple of jumps, the captain unrolled the decaying, yellowed, moth-eaten map he'd followed. Jackson had found it in a treasure chest near the beach shantytown where they'd materialized at the start of the match, but it'd taken far too long to decode the directional glyphs and align them properly with the apparent noonday sun to understand where they were and where they needed to go.

That was the exact kind of puzzle delay he'd hoped his extra training would eliminate. If they'd deciphered it sooner, they wouldn't have to deal with the enemy team. The map indicated a ship near the center of the fleet, but with their opponents on their heels, the Cardinals had very little time.

Adrien stuck the map into his pocket and glanced over his shoulder. Four forms vaulted onto another galleon a few ships back. They conjured spinning bolas and launched them, but the Cardinals dodged the attack easily. The Orono players couldn't realistically blow away every ship in sight given that they were behind their rivals, and they didn't want to risk damaging the ship containing the token. The Cardinals, on the other hand, didn't have a problem cutting off their own retreat.

The Charlottesville players sprinted toward the aft of their current ship before they burst onto the next closest galleon and launched a few fireballs behind them. Shadowy mists coalesced on the deck and flowed into humanoid shapes.

The Light Elf conjured a sword and pointed to the ship behind him. "Hilda and Carlos with me. Dennis and Marcus, sink that ship and keep the other team busy."

Dennis saluted with a grin. "Aye, aye, captain." He spun and raised his wand.

Adrien charged forward and raised his sword. Skeletal pirates, complete with ragged shirts, boots, and bright red headscarves tied around their skulls, stepped out of the mists. Sabers materialized in their hands. Dozens now blocked the team's passage, and there was no way they could get close enough to burst onto the other ship without fighting through the ghostly crew.

Fireballs erupted from the wands of the two teammates behind them. One spell exploded against the base of a mast to crack and weaken it. Another struck the ship near the waterline. The wizards fired again and raised a cloud of smoke but didn't deliver a decisive blow. The kind of vessel that could take multiple cannonballs wouldn't be felled by a few junior wizard attacks.

Hilda's summoned chain wound around a skeleton. The monster collapsed into a pile of bones, and the chain fell to the deck. A second later, the bones formed back into its full form and it picked up its saber.

"That's annoying." Carlos blasted one with a fireball,

but other than scorching the pirate's sash and bone, he didn't slow it.

Adrien rushed forward and swung boldly with his sword. His foe met his blade with his own and the resounding clang of metal on metal signaled the beginning of the bout. After exchanging a few swings and a quick step, he slashed at his opponent's neck and decapitated him. The skull bounced on the deck and the remaining bones turned to dust. The saber fell into the dust.

"Aim for the necks," he shouted.

Thick black and gray smoke poured from the burning galleon behind them. One of the masts fell, snagged the sails of a second, and ripped the already weakened wood down with it.

Adrien carved his way through boney pirates while Hilda and Carlos delivered precise fire and air blasts at the necks of the skeletons. Fine gray dust and swords now covered the deck.

"Dennis and Marcus, form up," the captain yelled.

The two other players bolted from their destruction of the now half-sunken galleon to join their team. They made it only about halfway before four of the Orono players careened through the smoke seconds later and landed near the angled, sinking deck of the burning galleon. Finn's absence disappointed Adrien, but the numerical inferiority of their opponents was welcome. He returned his attention to fighting skeletons as they needed to reach the next ship.

Marcus rattled off a blinding spell. A twirling rainbow orb erupted from his wand and exploded in a blinding shower of sparks. He groaned loudly, as did Dennis. Both put a hand to their eyes.

The Orono players tumbled wildly, their limbs flailing. One poor wizard's stomach caught the deck railing and he slipped into the ocean with a scream. The three others landed roughly, rolled, and groaned.

The elf gritted his teeth as he demolished another skeleton and looked over his shoulder. This had been a minor problem with some of the less experienced players. They got too excited and forgot to protect themselves from their own spells or to warn their teammates. At least Dennis had disabled the enemy team.

"Dennis, Marcus, hold Orono here," he shouted.

"I can't see anything," Dennis yelled back.

"When you can see, obviously." He snorted. Even championship teams stumbled. "Hilda, go help them." He sliced through a couple more adversaries. "All you have to do is help them pin Orono here. We're so close. Carlos, with me."

A huge golden Kraken statue perched atop a squat circular stone in the center deck of the next galleon. A chest covered in mother-of-pearl rested directly in front of it. It was on the exact galleon the map indicated. X marked the spot.

Hilda turned with a grin. She raised her wand and shouted her incantation. A cold mist swirled in the area and ice formed on the deck. The new frigid wall grew with each passing second.

Adrien shoulder-checked a skeleton pirate and sent the monster into the sea to provide calcium for a shark. Carlos launched three into the ocean with a quick push spell. Both Cardinals reached the aft of the ship and burst over to the next galleon.

The witch had no sooner finished a decent wall when an explosion blew chunks of ice from the side. Orono might be half-blind, but they weren't ready to give up.

Carlos turned and raised his wand. "I'll help Hilda if they get through. You get the token."

The elf nodded and sprinted toward the Kraken statue, his sword in hand. If more monsters appeared, his teammate was close enough to reinforce him. He snickered as he noticed the exquisite detail of the statue.

"Poor Montreal," he murmured. "Too bad they didn't make it to the quarter-finals." He tossed his sword into his other hand and knelt beside the chest. Hilda's wall shattered under a volley of blasts and sprayed the other galleon with ice chunks and steam.

Adrien gripped the lid and tried to lift it, but it was jammed.

"You have to be kidding me." He slipped his sword into a small crack between the lid and the body of the chest and pushed down hard.

Shouts sounded behind him as he pried the lid open. The best treasure in the world lay at the bottom—a gleaming Louper token.

He tossed his sword aside and snatched the prize. Triumphant, he stood and turned. "The quarter-finals are ours!"

CHAPTER SIXTEEN

Evie sighed as she approached Dorvu, a small dark jar of green frosted glass in her hand. The silver dragon lay coiled under the dappled shade of a tree, his eyes closed and his head resting on his forelegs. He cocked an eye open.

"A senior who dares to take a break?" The dragon chuckled lightly. "It's such a beautiful day. Good for you. So many of you are running around in a panic." He tilted his head up to stare at the cloudless sky. "The sun feels good on my wings when I fly. Perhaps I'm wasting my day lying here."

"I'm not taking a break exactly." She glanced at the jar. "I have a favor to ask, and it's somewhat personal. I'd ask someone else, but it has to be a dragon and you're the only one I know."

"Personal? And you need a dragon, you say?" He tilted his head and regarded her curiously. "No dark wizards are following you, are they? Or Black Dogs? Or anything else sinister and inappropriate?" He shook his head. "I'll protect you, but it's important to let the headmistress know. The school is much safer these days, but bad people always do have a way with tricks. I can't agree to keep quiet."

"Oh, it's nothing like that." She uttered a nervous laugh. "I'm doing extra-curricular potions work with Professor Fowler and she's had me collecting ingredients for this special portion all semester. I only have a few ingredients left to pre-treat, and you can help me with one of the most important."

"Potions ingredients?" He blinked. "I don't know a lot about that, Evie."

She lifted the jar so he could see it. "So…uh, here's the thing. I need a quarter-gallon—" She sighed. "I need a quarter-gallon of dragon saliva."

Dorvu nodded. "That's not such a discomforting thing, but it will be difficult for me to produce that much in human form. Maybe I should find some steaks to get my mouth going."

Evie shook her head. "Professor Fowler was very insistent that it had to come from you as a dragon. She said the saliva reacts differently based on your form."

"Oh. Well, then. That'll be easy. I have a lot more saliva as a dragon than in my human form." He pointed with his nose and his nostrils flared. "Set the jar down, and I'll give you all the saliva you need. I'd waste it by swallowing it anyway. You might as well do something useful with it."

She set the jar down and managed to restrain a laugh. Her ultimate potions project rested on having a dragon spit into a jar.

Evie smiled as she examined each vial and jar on the table in front of her. The potion would be the single most complicated she had ever brewed. It required dozens of ingredients, and she was now going through the process of confirming each ingredient and checking them off on a paper checklist Professor Fowler had given her.

"...Starflower petals, check. Gold nuggets, check. Platinum shavings, check. Infusion crystals. Dragon saliva." She sighed. "Check."

She glanced at a small vial containing the viscous fluid. Dorvu had been very accommodating, but that didn't make watching a dragon spit any less disgusting. Then again, they had no problem when he made ice for them, and that was almost like he was throwing up.

Evie grimaced. There were some things a witch simply shouldn't think about too much.

Professor Fowler folded her hands behind her back. She stood in front of the table with a smile. "The mass minion potion is cumbersome, I do admit, and in practical terms, the cost of the resources of those alone might be better suited for other potions, but I do think it's very important in that it reinforces the synergy of different ingredients and techniques. That is one of the major reasons why I selected it for your final project."

She frowned. "So you're saying no one would normally bother with this potion?"

"It's more impressive than it is useful in many situations, I imagine, but it's not useless either. It's merely cumbersome, as I said, and there are more efficient ways to accomplish the same thing with far fewer ingredients and steps." The professor shrugged. "But if you isolate any of the principles involved in its creation, you can see how they might benefit other potions. For example, think of how the power of infusion crystals can cross-react with certain types of herbs and metals in a way that makes them much, much more powerful." She pointed to a small jar containing translucent blue crystals suspended in a thick yellow-green liquid. "Consider that in the future. Infusion crystals are far easier to find and cheaper than many other types of amplification crystals. But, of course, using them means you're committing to a considerably longer potion preparation process."

Evie nodded. "And, you're sure the creatures made by this potion are only automatons, right?" She grimaced. "I don't want to accidentally create anything truly alive."

Professor Fowler gestured to the paper holding the recipe, which lay on the side of the table. "Glorified statues, nothing more. Note that if you go through every single one of those ingredients and think about how they work and the kinds of potions they are used in, you don't find anything directly related to the influence of souls." She smiled. "I'll admit that this isn't the only one I could have chosen to highlight the relevant techniques."

"Oh? Why else did you pick it then?"

"You and your friends do have a tendency to get into trouble. I know you're graduating soon, but I suspect you're the type who will end up never knowing when a mass minion potion might be helpful. Keep it on you, use it in a few years when you need help, and remember me fondly."

She laughed. "I think if I run into that kind of trouble as a potions witch apprentice, I'm doing something wrong."

"Perhaps." The professor tapped the recipe. "We've spent half this semester gathering the ingredients and beginning pre-treatment. It'll take most of the rest of the semester to continue processing and actually brewing the potion." She chuckled. "So try to not get into any trouble anytime soon if you can help it."

"I'll keep that in mind, but I don't think there'll be trouble."

"It has a tendency to sneak up on us when we least suspect it." Professor Fowler frowned. She crouched until she was eye-level with a jar filled with sunflower seeds and pointed to it. "You soaked these in the wrong solution."

Evie gasped. "I did?"

"Yes." She tapped the jar. "If you look at your notes, you'll see that once you soak them, they should develop a light luminescent sheen. You'll need to get more seeds and treat them for at least one evening under full moonlight. Fortunately, the moon cycle has worked in your favor."

"I'm sorry." Evie sighed. "I can't believe I screwed that up."

"Don't worry. We all make mistakes, but it's important to double-check not only the collection of the ingredient but also the pre-treatment." She pointed to the dragon saliva. "That's a good quantity, and I see you've kept it out of too much direct sunlight after the pre-treatment."

She made a face. "Thanks. I have a long future ahead of me in collecting weird things from strange creatures."

"For many potions, yes. I've always specialized in plant-based potions, but you never know when you can use some good dragon drool."

CHAPTER SEVENTEEN

Sara held her breath as she led Madelyn into the back of the Art Room. Her heart thundered and her palms grew sweaty. She'd finished the painting, and despite how grateful the other girl had been when she'd mentioned the project, there was always the chance she would hate it. Some artists might not care what people thought of their work, but she definitely wasn't like that.

There were many different reasons a person might respond poorly to a painting, from the aesthetic to the emotional, and this work wasn't merely a normal painting. Sara took a deep breath.

Why had she ever thought this was a good idea? She was good at painting, but that was far from having the skill necessary to produce such a complicated emotional work in a tasteful way. The entire thing might prove to be a horrific mistake.

They passed tables and shelves filled with drawing pads, pottery, paintings, sculptures, and even a few bonsai trees. Different people had different views on how to interface with the artistic soul. All might vary in the technical particulars, but all were valid.

The kitsune stopped in front of her easel in the back of the room. A small sheet hung over the painting. She almost turned Madelyn around and declared the whole thing a mistake. After a few more deep breaths, she summoned her courage.

"I didn't want to show you this while I was working on it because I thought it would have more impact if I showed you when I'd finished it, but I did take into account what you told me before. I did the joint painting rather than the two separate portraits, and like I mentioned, it does include some motion magic. Nothing serious or complicated. I've enchanted limited control verbal commands into it, so if you need to take pictures or something and are having trouble, it's not hard. It's actually quite interesting magic, and doing this project helped me improve my skill with that sort of thing."

Sara knew she was babbling at that point, but her courage failed her again and she tried to find a way to delay having to reveal the picture. Although she'd worked on several paintings that meant something to other people, this was her first attempt at a memorial work, and any failure would strike deeply not only into her heart but also her intended recipient's. She might even offend or hurt Madelyn—the ultimate failure.

The Coral Elf nodded, her curious gaze fixed on the sheet.

"Technically, it's not a portrait since it's a wider scene with two people—and motion, too." She frowned. "So I want to make that clear. If you tell someone it's a portrait, they'll be confused, and that's my fault because I kept using the term portrait. I don't want you to feel bad because I misled you about the kind of painting I would create. You could be having a discussion, and you point to the painting, and then people are like, 'What are you talking about? That's not a portrait.' Then, it's all a big mess. You know how people can be."

"I don't...know a lot of people who would say that sort of thing." Madelyn smiled. "I'm sure it's wonderful, Sara. You're such a talented artist and I don't believe you would paint me something I didn't like. It's why I was so happy when you approached me."

The kitsune chuckled and tried to conceal the slight panic building in her. "Oh, I paint my fair share of stinkers, and I've had to put in considerable practice to get this far. I'm not saying this one is bad, only that...I'm not perfect as an artist, which is why I'll study art for another four years after graduating." She took another deep breath, "But I suppose I should simply get on with it and show you the painting and stop trying to put everything in context. It's a painting, not a song or a poem. It's not like you'll need any interpretation help. The eyes don't lie and all that." She reached toward the easel but hesitated and her hand hovered over the sheet. "I present to you, *Sisters.*" She yanked the sheet off and sucked in another deep breath.

In the painting, Vianna and Madelyn stood together in front of a tall willow tree, its leaves gone, surrounded by piles of snow on the ground. The motion began with a light breeze blowing snow into drifts. Vianna grinned and sneaked behind her sister to grab a handful of snow in her mitt-covered hand. Madelyn turned and gasped in mock surprise, her hand over her mouth. Her sister dropped the snowball and pulled her into a hug. The painting stopped moving.

Sara continued to look at the artwork, too afraid to check on her companion's reaction. She hadn't been this nervous about one of her works in a while. Maybe ever.

"So, it'll stay on this final image for a minute and then reset," she said. "You can say the title and 'continuous' if you want it to constantly cycle or the title and 'freeze' to stop it at any particular point. It shouldn't blur or anything. It's magic, not a movie." She rubbed the back of her neck. "Now I wonder if I messed up."

"Why would you say that?" Madelyn said quietly from behind her and her voice wavered.

The kitsune winced. The Coral Elf must be furious to speak in that kind of tone. "I didn't ask you about what kind of scene you wanted. After you told me you wanted a joint picture, I jumped to a playful scene, but I never thought to ask you about what you might have preferred. It's supposed to be something important to you, so I should have sought your input. I'm sorry. I was arrogant and pushed my artistic vision onto something that's supposed to be a gift for you. That's not fair, and I don't know what else to say other than I'm deeply, deeply, sorry." She turned to face her.

The girl stood there in silence. Her eyes glistened, and thick trails of tears trickled down her cheeks. "You don't understand." She walked past Sara and reached toward the painting but stopped before she touched it. "Can I...touch it? Or will that ruin the paint?"

Sara shook her head. "No, it's fine. I wouldn't touch it

all the time or anything, but it's dry if that's what you're asking."

Madelyn rested her finger on Vianna's head. "I wish I could explain to you to make you understand. We use the word sister, but that's incomplete. It doesn't really describe what I had with Vianna. We were two halves of the same soul—one whole split in two. That made us...closer than you could ever truly understand or imagine. Even now, I wake up and I feel the pain of her absence. It hurts knowing she'll never come back." Her voice was soft and almost pleading.

"I-I'm sorry." Sara looked down. "I meant to do something I thought you would like. I-I'm sorry. I really am."

"No." The Coral Elf turned to face. "You still don't understand. I love it. It makes me feel like she's here with me again. I've thought about her a lot. I thought she was mean to me sometimes, but she loved me. She always tried to protect me and even planned to save me at whatever cost from the beginning." She sucked in a breath. "I understand so much more now than even when she died, let alone when we first came to Earth. If I knew what would happen, I would have done more to get mementos of her. So, thank you. This is special to me, and I'll treasure it."

Sara blinked a few times. "You're welcome."

Madelyn gave her a light hug before she pulled away. She blinked a few times. "I need to process things for a little while and get my tears under control, but I'll come back tomorrow to pick it up if that's okay."

"No, that's fine. I'll let everyone else in Art Club know in case you need help."

"Thank you." She wiped her tears on her sleeve and headed toward the door.

Sara took a deep breath and released it slowly as a smile crept onto her face. She now understood the value of her upcoming stint in art school a little better. An artist always wanted to touch others with their work, but her years at the School of Necessary Magic had been defined by adventures with the Trouble Squad and her difficulties with her magic. Even with the paintings she'd done for others, she'd let herself forget about how important a meaningful piece of art could be. In the right circumstances, it could change a person's life in a lasting way.

She wiped a happy tear away. Madelyn now had a piece of her sister that would last her for the rest of her life, and Sara had made that happen. Even with Hideki's painting the previous year, she didn't feel as if she'd so fundamentally touched another person's soul.

"I love being a painter."

CHAPTER EIGHTEEN

Raine grabbed a handful of stale popcorn and munched on it as the credits rolled for their latest movie, *The Happening*. They were definitely in a rough patch now, depending on who you asked. There had been a tense discussion of *The Village* two movie nights before, with Adrien, of all people, mounting a passionate defense of the movie's themes of deceiving people for their own good and how that could backfire. He even suggested a potential link to how magic was kept secret, even though Shyamalan had made no public statements suggesting a link to a magical family or any knowledge of true magic before the gates began to open. By the end, he had convinced Cameron, Evie, and Raine of the artistry of the film, whereas Madelyn, Sara, Philip, and William insisted it was nothing more than a cheap bait and switch.

When they had rolled onto *Lady in the Water* during their previous movie night, only Madelyn liked the film. She presented the argument that she could relate to a semi-aquatic woman from another world who was being hunted by forces she couldn't stop without the help of a diverse group of friends. Raine appreciated the fantastical nature of the story but couldn't quite get over the fact that the director basically cast himself as a prophet whose artistic work would change the world. Even under the kindest of interpretations, it came off as pretentious.

That brought them to *The Happening* in which Shyamalan returning to something approaching more basic horror. It also was his first R-rated film.

"I honestly don't know how I feel about it," Philip said and shook his head. "And this is the second time I've seen it. The idea of nature going after humanity is kind of cool, and I liked that it was good, old-fashioned horror rather than him pontificating about stories or trying to make some big sociological statement, but it didn't do it for me. I wondered if I'd missed something the first time, but I didn't."

Cameron nodded. "The tone is uneven. It jumps around, and some of the tropes are so forced it hurts to watch. It's like he had a checklist of 'These are things you must have in your creepy movie' and put them in there regardless whether they made sense or not. The old lady was too much for me. She was funny, not scary. Much it was, actually. He tried hard for most of 'the real monsters are people when they're scared,' but the rest of the premise undermines it and most of the deaths didn't carry any weight. Again, it's a checklist thing. 'Oh, now I need to do something awful to really drive home how bad everything is.' It's hard to believe this was directed by the same man who put something together so well-constructed and creepy as *The Sixth Sense*."

Raine sighed. "I rather liked it. It had its flaws, I admit, but there were some parts that really got to me. I felt bad for some of the characters, so that has to count for something. I agree that many parts were stupid and didn't make all that much sense, but I didn't find it as painful as *Lady in the Water*."

Sara frowned. "I like Mark Wahlberg as an actor in films from that era, but let's be real. That guy doesn't play a credible science teacher. I kept half-thinking they would reveal he was a fake teacher or only filling in for someone that day or something. I didn't think he had good chemistry with Zooey Deschanel either. I've liked her in other stuff, both from that era and her super-serious historical drama stint in the 2030s, but in this movie, I found her annoying."

Adrien snorted. "The characters aren't even the worst problem. I think they needed to decide what kind of movie they wanted. On one level, it felt like they tried to base it around a serious message concerning environmental destruction, but the execution of the cheap horror stuff interferes with that. Honestly, they didn't align it well." He frowned. "The way people were affected didn't feel like a revenge of nature plot. It merely felt like a cheap excuse for a higher rating. Everything felt so random." He shook his head. "I don't mind films where a lot of people die in gruesome or disturbing ways, and I can even appreciate the artistry of one that is well done, but this didn't feel well done. It felt forced and cheap. Most of the deaths also stopped being surprising early in the film, so the later deaths had zero impact for me."

William shook his head. "I can see all that, but I was

creeped out in a few places, so it works on that level. I'm not saying you guys are wrong to have your reactions, but I'd be a little creeped out if I saw swaying trees."

Cameron snickered. "You shouldn't be afraid of trees. You're half-Ifrit. You can burn them down. What would I do? Claw them until they fall?"

Everyone shared a laugh.

Madelyn scratched her cheek, her brow furrowed in thought. "I-I agree with Adrien. Maybe it's strange for me of all people to say this after defending *Lady in the Water*, but it didn't feel realistic, and the ending was too abrupt and went against the rest of the movie. Does that make sense?"

Evie nodded. "I get what you mean. It didn't feel like all the emotional buildup really paid off. I didn't care about the main characters that much anyway, to be honest, but if I had, the ending would have been annoying because of what it implied."

The shifter scoffed. "The ending was a cheap copout. He couldn't decide if he wanted a happy ending or a bad ending, so he has that fake-out with, I guess, the final scene being his twist or whatever. I hate that kind of thing. It feels lazy. I hate it in other movies, too. Don't build your entire movie in one direction to make some emotional point and then suddenly invalidate everything that happened for a cheap shock at the end. It's not clever or subversive. It's simply lazy as opposed to something like *The Cabin in the Woods* that at least tried to say something about horror and bad endings."

"To be fair," Philip said. "That movie was supposed to be

a satire of certain types of horror films, so it did go in a different direction."

"Satirical or not, it was still a way better horror flick than *The Happening*. Maybe he tried to be funny or satirical, but I doubt it. Everything's played so straight and deadly serious."

"It might be better as a remake," Raine said. She shrugged as everyone turned to look at her. "Adrien's right about the fundamental theme being interesting, but when the movie was made, most people didn't know about magic. Shyamalan obviously isn't afraid of magic and fantasy in his stories, but maybe he wanted to get away from it for a while. I think if he'd leaned into that sort of thing in this movie, it could have benefited it, rather than the really weird and forced semi-scientific explanation."

"What do you mean?" Cameron asked. "How would adding magic possibly help this movie?"

"Think about *Lady in the Water* and all those fantasy elements. He used them in service of a story about art, basically, but here, if he wanted to tell a horror story featuring the environment and really didn't want it to be all that much about the environment in some serious thematic sense, he should have used antagonists that parse their motives more directly. Like vengeful dryads or Wood Elves or something. It might make the whole thing feel more grounded and give the deaths more weight."

Adrien snickered. "Ah, it'd be nice to see Wood Elves take a little mud in humans' movies for the change. It's always the stuck-up Light Elf who needs to learn a life lesson, I swear, or who won't accept the advice of the worldly-wise human." He rolled his eyes and shook his finger. "And don't say a thing about me being stuck-up."

Cameron laughed. "Most werewolf movies that come out still have wolf shifters as vicious killers. Maybe because of the success of *Wolf of my Dreams* this year, that'll change, but I doubt it."

Raine sighed. "I still think it would have been a more interesting movie if the threat wasn't so abstract. They kept saying it was about balance or whatever, but it might as well have been random killer clouds."

Philip popped a chip in his mouth and crunched. A few bites later, he swallowed. "Oh, well. We all knew we would hit this rough patch. Better luck next time."

CHAPTER NINETEEN

Days later, the three FBI Trouble Squad couples wandered down a narrow row of clothing shops in the kemana. Adrien again begged off the outing in favor of Louper practice, but given the way the season was going, no one could blame him. Due to the vagaries of the schedule, there was a long gap between the Cardinals' quarter-final and semi-final match, which provided more time for him to run the team through even more intense training.

The theme of the Spring Formal was supposed to be unconventional materials, but no one had been very clear on what that meant in terms of individual outfits or the application of magic.

Philip yawned. "I don't see why we needed to come dress shopping with you for the Spring Formal. Aren't we supposed to not see you until the day of the event or it's bad luck?"

Sara rolled her eyes. "That's wedding dresses, not dance dresses. Stop making new things up."

"Making up new things is fun, though."

Cameron nudged Raine. "I'm simply happy to be here when she's not looking for Thothites in every window."

William cleared his throat. "I…uh." He glanced over his shoulder and frowned. "I'm not saying it's Thothites, but we are being followed by someone. He's done a decent job of pretending not to follow us, but I spotted him several minutes ago."

The shifter laughed. "Good one."

The half-Ifrit boy continued frowning. "I'm not joking. We're being followed."

Evie moved closer to him and slid her hand to a pouch at her side. Although she had her wand underneath her jacket, a quick potion toss could disable a man quicker under the right circumstances.

Cameron's smile fell. "Seriously? I can't believe this. The one time we're *not* looking for trouble."

"No one look yet," Raine said. "I'll peek when we reach the intersection. It's more natural to look around at a place like that."

The six students continued to stroll down the street. They offered polite nods to a few vendors, including an overly enthusiastic gnome selling, by his own statement, previously cursed dolls. She didn't indulge her curiosity as to why someone would even want something like that. They arrived at the corner, and she glanced nonchalantly to her side. It was time to see who was following them.

Agent Connor had worked with both William and Raine that semester on collecting information with brief looks, both for perception training and to reinforce some of the limits of eyewitness testimony. The latter portion had dropped away as the two students became too good at quick observation. The FBI agent set up different objects or even dummies in the room, told them to look for a short moment, and quizzed them on what they had seen. She now wondered if he intended it for situations like their current predicament despite stressing to her that the FBI was more about careful investigation than high-octane shootouts and confrontations like those in the movies.

"Are you talking about the man in the navy-blue suit, William?" Raine murmured. "I peg him at about six feet, stocky, and maybe two hundred pounds. There are two obvious bumps, one low and one high, so I guess a pistol and a wand."

"Yes." William nodded. "That's the guy."

Cameron blinked. "Is Connor teaching you two to be FBI agents or Sherlock Holmes?"

She grinned. "Attention to detail is important for any investigator, and every FBI agent is fundamentally an investigator regardless of their particular assignment."

Philip licked his lips. "That's cool and all, but we're still being followed by a suspicious guy. Maybe Raine isn't wrong about the Thothites, after all."

"They aren't interested in us, though. They only care about Madelyn, and if they intended to target us, they had chances before, including many times when I was only with Cameron." She frowned. "But I'd like to ask him a few questions to be sure. He might only be a scout."

"We could get the Ruby Falls police," Cameron said.

"They'll drag him off too quickly. Let's catch him and then get the police." Raine nodded up the street. "There's that alley behind the transforming noodle shop. It loops around, remember?"

Cameron snorted. "Why do I have the feeling you've been running scenarios for months now on how to ambush Thothites?"

She shrugged. "It doesn't hurt to be aware of your surroundings and take note of them."

The students altered course and wandered toward the alleyway at a leisurely pace. Both Evie and Sara's hands hovered near their pouches. Philip's hands twitched, but he didn't draw his wand. Raine kept her hand down as well. Spooking their tail might send him elsewhere, and she wanted to get in at least a couple of questions before the police grabbed him.

"Just so you know, if this guy makes any moves, I'll bite his hand off." Cameron growled as if to punctuate the statement.

"That sounds fair."

Raine led the other five students into the alleyway. Cameron shifted in an instant. She and Philip drew their wands while Evie yanked out a small blue glass vial but kept her wand inside her jacket. Sara tugged an acorn from her pouch. William raised his hand and summoned a small flame in his palm. They waited and watched the far wall for the shadow of their tail.

A dark outline appeared on the wall, and they sprinted around the loop to come up behind the suited man.

Raine and Philip pointed their wands at him. Cameron bared his fangs and let out a long, low growl. Evie raised her arm, ready to throw the potion, and Sara cocked her arm as well. William raised his palm and nodded toward the flame.

"If Cina were here," Raine began in a stern tone, "she might be able to eliminate us all. She barely needs to move to cast her spells, but you're not Cina. You don't have your wand out nor your gun. If you make any sudden movements, my shifter friend here will bite your hand off. He just said so, and even if you could draw your wand or gun, there's no way you can get a decent spell or shot off before we take you down."

The man grimaced and raised his arms slowly as if pushing through molasses. "It's not what you think. I don't work for Cina."

She scoffed. "Why should we believe that?"

"Okay, I can see your position and why you might think that way, but let's not do anything hasty we regret." The man sucked in a breath. "My name is Agent Clemson. I'm with the PDA. I'll reach inside very slowly for my badge. How does that sound?"

Raine nodded. "Okay, but please don't do it quickly." The fire drained from her voice. If the man wasn't lying, there was no reason to be rude.

He inched his hand into his jacket and retrieved his wallet at a pace a snail would find embarrassing. Finally, he flipped it open to reveal a PDA badge.

The students lowered their weapons of choice and exchanged embarrassed looks. William's flame vanished. Cameron shifted into human form, an uneasy smile on his face.

"We're sorry, Agent Clemson," Raine said as she stowed

her wand inside her jacket. "We thought… Well, you know what we thought."

He rubbed the back of his neck. "I have to say I'm a little embarrassed, but I should have believed Agent Oliver."

"Why? What did she say?"

Agent Clemson shrugged. "She told me how impressive you all were, and how you were calmer and more collected in dangerous situations than half the agents she's known in the PDA."

Cameron frowned. "Why were you following us?"

"I'm looking into the Children of Thoth. I was curious as to whether they might be interested in you at all since you played a part in stopping them from kidnapping the girl the first time. And, I suppose, I wanted to test you. That last part's more the main reason, you could say. I thought I'd follow you for a while and see if you eventually caught on." He chuckled. "I didn't expect you to see me after only ten minutes."

"If you've followed us for ten minutes and I spotted you five minutes ago, it only took us five minutes to detect you," William said and raised his chin with pride. "I wanted to confirm we were being followed before I worried anyone else."

"Good job, kid. Given the fire I saw, you must be William, right?"

He nodded. "Yes. What about it?"

"Are you sure you want to join the FBI and not the PDA?" Agent Clemson grinned. "I won't even bother to ask Raine. Agent Oliver told me all about her FBI obsession."

The half-Ifrit shook his head. "I think I'll stick with the FBI."

"I'll simply say that you kids are a lot more impressive than I was at your age." He released a sharp breath. "Now that we have that settled, how about I follow you around a little in case we get lucky?"

Raine looked at her friends. They all nodded.

"We were just discussing how the Thothites have had more than enough opportunity to try something with us but haven't, but that's fine by us. It's your time."

CHAPTER TWENTY

The Thothites were pushed to the very back of Raine's mind as she swayed with Cameron to light orchestral music, dressed in a blue gown. Although the sheen, texture, and color of the fabric suggested a conventional dress with a midi skirt, the entire outfit was created from the silk of an insectoid species native to Oriceran whose name she couldn't even begin to remember let alone pronounce.

The rest of the Trouble Squad had adopted a similar approach to the unconventional materials theme and chose unusual fabrics that look normal. Many students, however, wore more visibly strange materials, including uncomfortable-looking bark, scale, and feather outfits, and made her question if she'd gone down the right path. Cameron merely wore a normal tuxedo, so she didn't really care when it came down to it. In the end, the only person's opinion at that dance she cared about was his.

He looked around, a slight frown on his face. "I'm almost surprised."

"Surprised at what?" she asked and mirrored his quick scrutiny of their surroundings. "All the outfits?"

"That, too, but mostly that you're so okay."

She cocked her head to the side and regarded him with bemusement. "Okay? Why wouldn't I be okay? I'm in a pretty dress, the music is pleasant, and I'm dancing with the best boy in this school. This is a great, enjoyable night in every way."

The shifter grinned. "I am pretty awesome, but I thought because Madelyn's not here, you might have been obsessing over her. I love that you care so much about other people, but you can't always shut it off even when it's for your own good."

"It's not like I always worry about her. If it's because this is a dance, Halloween was different." Raine shook her head. "The veil isn't thin in spring, and so there's no reason to worry. She's made it clear she won't leave campus until Cina is taken care of. Madelyn's fine, and I need to learn to let go as much as she needs to learn social skills." She took a deep breath. "I will admit I feel a special responsibility and not only because of the promise. You guys were all involved with Arc Eighty-Eight because of me, but I was one of the people Maeve was interested in. I've been at the center of this from the beginning and now, I feel that if I'd handled everything differently, this could have been resolved better to begin with."

Cameron frowned. "Don't torture yourself with what might have happened. You can't fix the past."

"I know, but it's hard not to think about it, especially since Maeve became two girls who simply wanted to live. I'm not saying I should have stayed with her to become her eternal friend or whatever, but if I only understood what I do now, I might have been able to help her. Because of that, I feel like I don't want to make the same mistake with Madelyn. I've been able to help her grow as a person, but there's still this threat hanging over her." She forced a smile. "Then again, I might be worrying too much. We're closing in on April, and nothing has happened. I'm beginning to think nothing will happen."

He grunted. "And that's a bad thing? If she's grown as a person, that's all you should really care about. The PDA, FBI, and police will capture Cina. If she's still hiding when you're an official agent, maybe they'll assign you to her case." He shrugged. "Or they'll catch her tomorrow, and you won't have to worry."

"I get that, and it's what I want. A resolution." She shrugged. "It's hard to let go of the problem when the threat is there, still close, and I know it might come back. I'm only glad that Madelyn is smart enough to avoid the kemana. I don't know if I'd be able to sleep at night if she risked herself there. It's not that I want her to be terrified. I simply want her to be safe."

The shifter offered a slight nod in response, concern in his eyes. Raine let the conversation lapse. They were supposed to simply have a good time together, not brood over situations neither of them could change.

She moved back against him and they swayed to the music without talking for a couple of minutes, simply holding each other close. The music faded, and another slow, orchestral piece started, this time accompanied by haunting ethereal notes in the melody.

Raine was no expert on Oriceran music, but she recognized at least one Light Elf instrument, a polyphonic flute. Every year, the cultures of Oriceran and Earth mixed more openly. The distinction between the two planets might fade away with enough time.

Cameron looked past her as if he saw something fascinating behind her.

"What's up?" Raine asked.

"Nothing. Why do you ask?"

"You suddenly seem a little distracted and not in the moment. Did I ruin the mood with all the Madelyn stuff?" She glanced around. Everyone was relaxed with smiles on their faces, an impressive feat considering that at least one couple wore matching outfits that appeared to be carved out of opaque ice. Magic radiated off them, so she wasn't sure if they used it to hold the outfits together or keep themselves from freezing.

"I'm here," he said softly. "I…I'm sorry. I'm pulling a Raine Campbell. I'm the one who brought her up, to begin with, and now, I'm the one who is overthinking something."

"What's on your mind? We can dance and talk at the same time."

He moved a hand from her waist to gesture around the room. "Maybe because this dance is such a milestone, it's really struck home that this is our last semester in a way it hasn't before. I'm comfortable with going to college and then the Secret Service, but I'm still adjusting to the idea of not being able to see you every day. It's one thing during the summer because I've always known that I'd come back to you soon, and now, that'll change. It's a lot to take in."

Raine's cheeks heated, and she looked down. "Even if

I'm assigned to the west coast, I'll only be a single train ride away. I know we'll have to do some creative schedule juggling at first, but we'll still be able to be together."

"I get that." Cameron chuckled. "But it's not the same as knowing we'll eat together and go to class together every day. It's hard to face that reality. I'm not saying I can't handle it, but sometimes, the thought suddenly seems very real. You're the best thing to ever happen to me."

She sighed and looked away, her cheeks on fire. "I get it, but as long as we continue to take every opportunity, it won't be so bad. It won't be as good, but it won't be terrible, at least. Many people have long-distance relationships for a while."

The shifter smiled. "I know. This is only me pulling my ultra-loyal dog act. We should enjoy our last few months at the School of Necessary Magic and view it for what it is."

"And what's that?"

"Not an ending but the beginning of the rest of our lives." He inhaled deeply through his nose. "Being here has given us both so many opportunities, and it makes it pointless to have even come here if we don't go out and take advantage of those. Not only that, I'm grateful for this place every day, Raine, because if it wasn't for this school, I would have never met you. A future where I can't eat all my meals with you is an inconvenience, but the idea that we might not have been together is a nightmare."

Raine's breath caught. Her heart rate kicked up. "Cameron, I-I don't know what to say."

"I do. I love you, Raine. That's all I'm trying to say, and I know we'll work through whatever challenges face us in the future. If we can take on chaos witches, Willen criminals, and handle dangerous magical VR fairies, we can make a temporary long-distance relationship work." Cameron grinned. "It'll probably be the easiest thing we'll ever do together for the best payoff."

"You're right." She rested her head against his chest. "I love you, too, Cameron."

The couple swayed to the music and all the other people in the room faded into the dim background. For that night, they were twin stars destined to forever dance through the heavens together.

CHAPTER TWENTY-ONE

"I can't believe it," Sara muttered and shook her head. "I still can't believe it." She walked with Raine in Ruby Falls. They'd stepped out of a small shop selling Oriceran fruits, mostly colorful melons.

Raine glanced at the shelves in front of the shop. They contained various melons. The odd striations and colors of some of them gave her pause, but she hadn't grown up in the magical world and she was still shedding her non-magical instincts. There was no reason her friend should be shocked.

"What's wrong? Did you see moldy fruit?" She grimaced. "Do you see talking fruit? Singing fruit?"

The kitsune laughed and shook her head. "No, I didn't see anything like that. It's only…you don't get it, do you? You have no idea what I'm talking about."

"No, I don't." She frowned and made no effort to hide her confusion. "What should I know? I feel like I got lost in the middle of this conversation somehow."

"Last Sunday was April Fool's Day and nothing happened." Sara's eyes widened, and she nodded solemnly.

"And?" Raine shrugged. "You made it clear that you wouldn't participate in any prank wars."

Sara nodded. "Sure. I didn't participate, but it's not like the Live Unnecessary Tricksters are focused only on me. It's not that they didn't prank me but that I didn't hear about them pulling any pranks. Did you?"

"Huh. Now that I think about it, you're right. Maybe they only want to do it during class."

"Then they could have done it sometime last week." Her companion shook her head. "Nope. No prank war this year. Maybe my speech to Jillian convinced her to channel herself in another way."

"It could be."

They turned a corner, and Raine sighed. A thin man in a dark suit had tailed them for several minutes. She didn't notice any obvious bulges in his jacket.

"What's wrong?" the other girl asked.

"Cameron will be irritated when I tell him I went to the kemana and I was followed and he wasn't here to growl at the guy."

Sara snickered. "Then don't tell him. It's probably Agent Clemson again, trying to be slick."

"But he looks different."

"He bought a clue and is using illusion magic." The kitsune shrugged. "It's obviously not the Thothites. They won't show up and target you months after the fact when they could have before, and they'd probably do a better job of hiding. They've lived here for a while and know Ruby Falls."

She sighed. "You're right. Maybe Agent Clemson wanted to see if we would identify him in a different form."

"Let's give him a good day. We can pretend we don't see him so he'll think he's some master of disguise." Sara grinned.

Raine laughed. "There's a low-effort way to make someone feel good. Fine. I'm in."

The girls continued their stroll down the street and meandered in the general direction of the kemana entrance. Their tail remained entirely focused on the pair. A part of her was almost insulted that the man couldn't at least pretend he wasn't following them.

She was about to say as much when they turned a corner and passed the herbalist shop where Hap worked. The ferret wasn't stocking the outside shelves that day, but they'd seen him during another recent kemana visit. He continued to adjust well to his new career.

Raine glanced over her shoulder and blinked. "Huh. Maybe we were wrong."

"What?" Sara stopped and frowned. "About what?"

She pointed down the street. "He's gone. He must have simply been going in the same direction."

A strangled cry of anguish sounded from behind a small blue shop.

"What was that?" both girls asked in unison. They exchanged glances and rushed behind the building.

Raine pulled her wand out and cast a quick shield spell before they turned the corner. She gasped. She had been prepared for a horrific sight, including a murder victim or some bizarre Oriceran species she had never encountered, but she wasn't prepared for the suited man covered in feathers and egg yolks, including a couple that slid down his head.

She lowered her wand and burst out laughing. Sara stared at him for a moment before she joined her friend's amusement.

The man's shoulders slumped, and he shook his head. "It's not fair." His form shimmered and twisted for a moment before it reverted to a young brown-haired wizard in a T-shirt and jeans.

The kitsune narrowed her eyes. "Hey, I know you. You're a Trickster."

Movement caught Raine's attention, and a robed figure rushed around the opposite corner of the building, clutching a necklace.

"Who is that?" she pointed at fleeing figure.

"Jillian," the boy said glumly.

"What the heck?" Sara frowned. "Why are two Tricksters following me around?"

He nodded. "Today's the prank war. Jillian said we were too predictable, that April Fool's Day should be an inspiration, not a straitjacket. She said we could only understand the true nature of a prank if we weren't stuck in our ways. To avoid that, she said that we should do the prank war around April Fool's every year, but not on it. We tossed dice to determine if it'd be before or after and how far, and we came up with today as the choice."

Raine nodded when she heard the information. "That all makes sense." She snickered again as yolks slid down his shirt before she cleared her throat and locked a serious interrogatory expression on her face. "But what do we have to do with any of this? You were obviously following us, and you even went to the trouble of a disguise. Was Jillian following us as well?"

"Yes, Jillian is. All the Tricksters are." The boy shook his head. "But you're not involved, Raine." He nodded at Sara. "She is."

The kitsune frowned. "How am I involved? I specifically said I didn't want to be in a prank war. I made the very clear, and now, all the Live Unnecessary Tricksters are after me?"

"Jillian says you're a kitsune and your trickster spirit shouldn't be ignored out of fear. You're the embodiment of everything we aspire to be. Your magic is trickster magic."

"That's not her decision to make." Sara threw her hands up in irritation. "I can't believe this. So, what? You were stalking me to prank me?"

"Not exactly." The boy looked down, a sheepish smile on his face. "Kind of? We've called it a special prank war, the Kitsune Hunt. We're all supposed to follow you and prank each other. We have to defeat each other before the survivor goes after you. When we successfully prank someone, we collect their necklace to prove it, as well as any they might have won from others. If you prank someone else, you collect all necklaces from them. We know that once we have enough necklaces, we can go after you."

She groaned. "If I go back to the school, will they all lay off?"

He squared his shoulders. "I can't dishonor the hunt by spilling Trickster secrets."

"Fine," the kitsune snapped. "Be that way. This is stupid." She flicked her wrist in dismissal.

The boy jogged away, fear on his face.

Sara pinched the bridge of her nose. "I understand that pranks are important to Jillian, but I thought she understood where I was coming from."

"I don't think she's trying to be mean, and in a way, I think this is her way of trying to be a friend to you. She simply doesn't grasp that having trickster magic doesn't mean you want to be a Trickster in their sense." Raine sighed. "I'm not saying it's all right for her to ignore what you want, but I do understand the idea that last year was a weird situation, and she doesn't want to be limited by it."

"So what do I do?" Her friend glanced irritably around her and pursed her lips in annoyance. "They're obviously following me here, and I don't know how many Tricksters are left in the hunt. If I go back to school, I could hide in my room or maybe the library. There's no way they would dare pull a prank in there, and I don't know how they would manage it with the gnome brigade keeping a watchful eye on their domain."

She shrugged. "Who knows? I hate to say it, but they might want you to go back to the school. The professors tolerate their pranks, but people in Ruby Falls might not be so willing if there's collateral damage."

Sara closed her eyes and took a deep breath. "Let's head back to the school. At least that way, some random innocent person doesn't end up with egg on their face."

Raine looked away and put a hand over her mouth to hide her smile. Last year, she had been hurt by the chaos-magic tainted prank gone awry, but it was hard to muster the same concern about feathers and eggs.

CHAPTER TWENTY-TWO

A few minutes later, Raine blinked. A familiar girl walked along the street, her hands tucked in the pockets of her jeans—Erin.

"She's not a Trickster, is she?" she asked.

Sara shrugged. "I haven't seen her hanging around any of the Tricksters, but maybe they recruited her. They're always looking for new members."

"From what Madelyn's said and my few conversations with her, Erin doesn't seem a good candidate." She frowned. "Come on. Let's ask her directly." She jogged toward the blonde freshman.

The girl's eyes widened and her gaze darted nervously, and for a moment, Raine thought she would run.

"Hey, Erin." She smiled at the student. "Are you here by yourself?"

"Don't turn me in." Erin swallowed. "I know I'm not supposed to be in the kemana as a freshman. I get that. Totally."

The two friends exchanged looks.

Sara shrugged, a relaxed smile on her face. "Are you a Trickster?"

"Huh?" The girl blinked. "You mean like a jester or something?"

"No, a member of the Live Unnecessary Tricksters? Semi-secret society?"

"Wait." She shook her head. "Those are the guys who prank people, right? No, I'm not a member. I don't even like pranks. I think they're mean."

The kitsune nodded. "Okay, you might want to head back to the school, then."

Erin looked down and nibbled her lip. "But I want to spend time in the kemana. I've only gone a few times, and it sucks because Madelyn can't come. I don't really like the other girls whom I've gone with the last few times, so I decided to go by myself today."

"We're not telling you to go back because it's the kemana," Raine said. "We used to come to the kemana all the time when we were freshmen. It's more that the Live Unnecessary Tricksters are in the middle of a prank war, and although they're allegedly focused on Sara, you don't want to get caught up in it."

The younger girl winced. "Oh. Okay, I'll run to Bubble & Fizz for a snack and I'll come right back. It's kind of my reward for doing well on my last potions exam."

Raine shrugged. "Be careful. Although I would recommend not coming here by yourself. It's not like it's all that dangerous, but there are many con artists and that kind of thing. Remember, there is strength in numbers."

"S-sure, sure." Erin sprinted away as if fleeing an angry dragon.

"She's almost as skittish as Madelyn used to be in some ways," Sara muttered.

"Yes and no." She watched as the girl almost ran into a witch leading a floating box lashed to her wand by a rope of light. "She seems a little afraid of us, but the old Madelyn couldn't have come here by herself." She sighed. "Let's get out of here before a real Trickster comes."

Back on the school grounds, they skirted the trees, their assumption being that avoiding well-trodden paths would lower the chance of being pranked, but the continued mild sensation of magic behind her made Raine question their tactics.

"There's someone following us," she whispered. "I think they're invisible."

Sara gave a slight nod. "I can feel it, too, but the magic level is low. Maybe not all of them?"

"It could be they are already down to the last Trickster, someone who could use decent, long-lasting stealth magic and keep up with us."

"It's probably Jillian, then." The kitsune narrowed her eyes. "Enough time might have passed for that, I suppose, if there were only a few of them left. He said Jillian got him, so maybe she defeated the others too."

"We could use magic pulses to triangulate where she is," Raine suggested. "I'm sure Professor Powell would be proud."

Her friend snorted. "Proud we used the techniques he taught us to catch a prankster rather than a dark wizard?"

"I think anything that involves the technique being used is probably a good thing by his standards." She shrugged.

"I have another suggestion. I don't want to play by these people's rules. They think they can stalk me and get away with it, even though I told Jillian I didn't want to be involved." Sara curled her hand into a fist. "I don't want to be their fun today. I want to defeat them."

Raine nodded slowly. The look of determination on her friend's face suggested more competitiveness than anger, but anything that didn't end with them getting egged and feathered was fine by her.

"What's your plan?" she asked.

Sara grinned. "They expect us to be careful. They probably even expect us to use magic to look for invisible Tricksters, but sometimes, the best strategy is the most obvious."

She thought about this for a moment and nodded. "We run?"

"Yep. We run." Her companion winked. "Meet you back at our room." She burst into a sprint and cackled with laughter.

Raine chuckled and ran after her. Sara's competitive spirit would always be a lighthearted and carefree source of amusement.

They huffed and puffed as they rushed away from the forest and across the verdant spring grass of Horace's well-maintained lawn. The groundskeeper waved at them in the distance, and they waved back but continued their sprint.

The magical presence behind them grew distant. Whoever was following them didn't keep up. The plan was working.

Her lungs strained as she continued to pump her legs to keep up with her friend. Sweat beaded on her forehead. The mansion grew closer and closer with each step that put them farther away from their invisible pranking nemesis.

"I…think…we're…escaping," she puffed.

Sara nodded, her face now almost as red as her hair.

All they had to do was make it to their room. Once they were safely there, they could hole up until dinner. The Tricksters almost always ended their prank wars in the late afternoon. Raine suspected they feared the wrath of an angry Headmistress Berens if they extended their games too far into the night.

The kitsune began to slow, her breathing ragged. Raine matched her pace. More magic flowed around them now as they reached the main mansion, but their opponent was probably halfway across the school grounds.

"Looks…like…we…win," she said.

Sara snickered and nodded. "Let's… get…inside."

By the time the two red-faced girls had reached their dorm room, they'd caught their breath. A few other students along the way eyed them curiously, but they didn't bother to explain why they looked like they'd fled from a horde of dark wizards. Given their reputations around the school, some students might have even assumed that and decided to leave well enough alone.

Raine took a deep breath and exhaled slowly. She reached for the door. "Now to stall until dinner."

Sara's eyes widened. "Wait!"

She had already grabbed the handle before her friend's warning. "What?"

"Don't you feel the magic?"

"There's always magic—"

Glowing slime winked into existence all around her. It circled her for a few seconds, almost hypnotic. She sighed and closed her eyes before it splattered over her body.

She groaned and wiped some of it out of her eyes. "I don't know if this is better or worse than eggs and feathers."

Sara yanked a single dried berry out of her belt pouch and threw it down the otherwise empty hallway. It exploded in a bright flash and a wave of energy surged along the hall. The floors warped and branches sprouted from the baseboards and thickened with leaves over a few seconds until a single person-shaped hole remained in the center.

Raine blinked. "Okay, that's new."

"I didn't think," the kitsune whispered. "I simply acted. Pure instinct."

A dark-robed Jillian winked into existence to fill the hole. Several necklaces hung from her neck. "Impossible."

"Impossible?" Sara scoffed. "We've beaten you before." She shook her finger. "And I'm still mad that you planned this even though I told you I didn't want to be involved."

The elf sighed and looked down. "You're right. I'm sorry. I only needed to be sure."

"Of what?"

"I'm not suppressing my precognition," Jillian said. "I'll admit it to the other Tricksters. It wasn't a fair contest, but

I wondered if I was wrong about everything—about the future, order, chaos—everything. I wondered if knowing the future meant I always could win, but you acted on pure instinct. I even saw it. I knew Raine would get slimed."

Raine groaned and shook slime off her hands. "Gee, thanks. I'm glad I could help you with your philosophical dilemma by getting coated in goo."

Jillian shook her head, wonder in her eyes. "I even knew Sara would throw the berry."

Sara smirked. "What? Not fast enough to dodge? So much for the power of precognition."

"No, it's because I didn't see..." She motioned around. "All of this. I saw a blinding spell from the berry." She removed all her collected necklaces and marched toward Sara, knelt, and laid the accessories at the other girl's feet. "We play at being Tricksters. We play at being unpredictable, but your kitsune trickster magic truly is unpredictable. I think...I've learned something important today. About the universe itself. About magic. About order and chaos."

"If you say so." Sara sighed. "I'm still mad, but because no one got hurt, I won't make a big deal about it. I don't feel as bad as I thought I would about participating." She ran her fingers along a nearby branch. "But get the rest of the Tricksters. If we clean this up right away, Headmistress Berens won't feed us to Dorvu."

The Gray Elf chuckled. "I've been lucky to be a Trickster while you were at this school, Sara."

"I'm not some avatar of chaos or whatever. I'm simply a girl who likes to paint."

"That and so much more." Jillian extended her hand. "I'm sorry. I won't do anything like that again."

The kitsune shook her head. "Good. I do understand why this is important to you, but..." She motioned around. "If you take anything from last year, remember that not all unpredictability is good."

Raine sighed. "I'm going to go get cleaned off. You guys can start the forestry cleanup without me."

CHAPTER TWENTY-THREE

Adrien shoved a muck-covered keycard through the rusty slot. The electronic lock emitted a harsh buzz. He didn't want to lose in the Louper semi-finals because he couldn't open a stupid magically locked door.

Hundreds of zombies now lumbered toward them with loud moans and their arms outstretched. Hilda led the other three players, who ripped chunks of concrete from the cracked streets and stacked them to create makeshift barriers and delay the progress of the horde. Destroying the creatures wasn't difficult if an attack delivered enough damage, but every time the team killed one, two new ones appeared on the edges of the mob.

"Maybe we'll get lucky and every Cincinnati player will get eaten," Carlos muttered.

A half-dozen locked doors leading into the moss-covered cement bunker barred farther passage through the simulated post-apocalyptic city. Garbage lay strewn about the streets and in front of buildings. Rusted cars jammed the street, and a brown haze kept the area dark. Anachronistic newspapers fluttered along in the breeze with the headlines: *ZOMBIES POUR OUT OF OPEN ORICERAN GATES!*

The captain had to give the match designers credit that season. They experimented with more cinematic themes in many matches, but he suspected that was part of the school leagues trying to align themselves with pro leagues and their attempts to attract an audience of game players.

He moved to the next lock and ran the card through. It beeped, and a bolt in the door retracted with a resounding thud. He pulled the door open and gestured inside the building. "Go."

The team broke away from their barrier and ran toward the door. Zombies began to crawl over one another in an effort to make it over the blockade. Their moans grew louder and more insistent.

Adrien spun inside and slammed the door shut. The bolt clunked again and echoed in the wide hallway where the Cardinals now huddled. Dim red emergency lighting softened the pitch-blackness barely enough for them to see.

"Are we sure this is the right place?" Hilda asked.

Adrien nodded. "If it wasn't, I doubt the keycard would have worked, and it matches the direction of the graffiti arrows we've found throughout the day." He summoned a light ball and a sword and pointed the blade at the side of the hallway. A faded red arrow lay on the wall, now fully visible in the full spectrum of the magical light.

The Cardinals nodded at their leader, and he rushed down the hallway, using his spell to better illuminate their path. As long as they didn't rely on the red emergency lighting, they could make out the directional arrows. The seconds flowed into minutes as they turned this way and that in the meandering corridor.

"Do you know what I realized?" Carlos said as they turned at another intersection. "I was joking before, but we haven't seen a single Lions player. If we can win this without even engaging them, it'll be technically our first shut-out of the season. It's funny that it wouldn't happen until the semi-finals."

Adrien nodded. "There are always ways to improve, even on apparent perfection, but we've not found the token yet. Let's not get ahead of ourselves. They might be saying the same thing and already be in the token room."

The team's trip dead-ended at a massive steel security door that stretched across the entire width of the hallway. Several keycards each labeled with a black number in a squarish font rested in a broken glass container on the wall. A metal mallet hung by a loose chain beside it.

The elf grabbed the keycards and frowned. "Two, three, five, seven, ten, thirteen, seventeen."

A small keycard slot stood on the side of the wall along with a flashing message on a screen beside it.

WARNING: EXPERIMENTAL CONTAINMENT FAILURE. AUTOMATED FAILSAFE IN EFFECT. NON-CORRECT KEYCARD USAGE WILL RESULT IN THERMAL CONTAINMENT PROTOCOL.

He frowned.

Hilda peeked over his shoulder. "What does that mean?"

"I think there's some kind of fire trap if we fail, but I don't understand what the numbers mean. There's a pattern there. Let's see. The numbers are one apart, then two apart, then two apart, then three apart twice…but then four apart? I don't get it. I need more of the sequence."

"No, you don't." Dennis' eyes widened. "It's the ten card. Use that one."

Adrien looked sharply at the wizard. "How can you be so sure?"

His teammate laughed. "Because you've made us read puzzle books this entire semester. Every other number in that series is a prime, except ten. It should have been two, three, five, seven, eleven, thirteen, seventeen."

"And you're sure?" He picked up the ten card. "If you're wrong, it might wipe the entire team out."

"I'm sure." Dennis nodded, conviction in his eyes.

Adrien rushed to the lock and ran the card through the slot. A pleasant beep sounded, and the entire hallway shuddered as the door retracted into the ceiling. Moans and groans suffused the hallway as the feet, bodies, and heads of zombies became visible.

The Cardinals didn't wait. They launched coordinated volleys of fireballs at the enemy until they winked out of existence, merely more casualties in the fake battlefield of a Louper match. By the time the door rose in full, the team had carved a path through the horde and to the token atop a dark lab bench in the center of the next room. There wasn't a single Lions player in sight.

"Go for it, Dennis," the captain said as he launched a fireball from his palm. "You earned it. Let's take our first complete shut-out."

The hulking wizard boy grinned and pointed his wand low as he crouched. A burst spell hurtled him through the gap toward the gleam of gold. Zombies shuffled from either side of the hole and turned toward him. Their moans echoed eerily in the cavernous chamber.

Despite a rough landing, he still ended up where he needed to be—in front of the lab bench. He snatched the prize. "Cardinals rule!"

CHAPTER TWENTY-FOUR

Philip held up a DVD. "The funny thing about this one is I don't think it ever came out on DVD. It was the first movie Shyamalan made after the opening of the gates, but he took some time off so there were a decent number of years before he made this one."

"Many people took breaks," William mumbled. "We might not have been alive, but it was a tough time for them. They had so much to adjust to."

Everyone nodded. They were happy to have made it through the rough patch, including the sad *After Earth* and back to better films over the last several movie nights, including the campy but enjoyable horror flick, *The Visit*. Everyone liked *Split* if only on the basis of James McAvoy's performance, but they had another mixed decision on *Glass*. Some, like Raine, liked the twist, but others like Adrien thought it was anticlimactic.

Raine pointed at the DVD. "*The True Elf*, right?"

Philip nodded and slipped it inside the player. "I haven't seen this one."

Adrien shrugged. "I have. It's okay. I'm unsure how I feel about what it's trying to communicate, but you can watch it and make your own mind up. At least it depicts Light Elves as heroic."

Everyone grabbed their snacks and settled in for the film.

It opened with a blond Light Elf in gleaming silver armor holding a massive sword that was almost as long as his body. An enormous dragon covered in dark obsidian scales filled the sky, it's body miles in length and its eyes covered in black smoke.

Text appeared on the screen.

In the ancient days on Oriceran, the elves stood against the darkness, including the embodiment of chaos, the Death Bearer. The sacred sword Light Bringer was bequeathed unto a new champion each generation, the only weapon capable of defeating the Death Bearer. This is the story of the thirteenth wielder of the Light Bringer, a Light Elf by the name of George.

Adrien cleared his throat. "I want to point out there's no such thing as a Death Bearer or the Light Bringer."

Sara rolled her eyes. "There's no such thing as narf or a scrunt, either. Just because it's set on Oriceran doesn't mean all the magic stuff has to suddenly be true."

"I only wanted to be clear. I don't want to spoil it, but it clarifies some of that later, and I didn't want you to be confused."

Philip put his fingers to his lip. "Shh. It's really starting now."

Most of the two hours passed with a fairly standard quest. After the opening, the story backed up to the death of the previous wielder of Light Bringer to reveal when she passed the sword to George.

Along the way, he dealt with accusations of the Death Bearer being a made-up threat, challenged by a gnome who called himself Mr. Reason. After the villainous darkness annihilated a village, George traveled through poisonous marshes and battled a variety of monsters on the way toward a cave. According to a Seer he met shortly after receiving the blade, the heart of darkness—representing the collected negative emotions of all beings on Oriceran—lay in the cave, and the only true way to slay the Death Bearer was to plunge Light Bringer into the heart.

The hero now crept toward the thumping blackened mass that filled the cavern, his sword before him, and the conversation with the Seer replayed in voice-over.

"Plunge the blade into the heart of darkness, and free the land from its own sins," the Seer intoned.

"Could it be that easy?" George shook his head. "I have trouble thinking it'll be a cakewalk. This will be easier than jaywalking on a busy New York street and not getting hit."

Raine frowned. "Is it only me or does George sound… weird? He sounds like someone from America, and in this movie, you don't even see Earth or any indication that the gates are open. He's also the only one making those kinds of references. Even his name seems off. There can't be many Light Elves named George."

"Maybe it's supposed to be symbolic because of the dragon-slaying Saint George," Philip suggested.

She shook her head. "Is the idea that the saint was supposed to be an elf?"

"Keep watching," Adrien murmured.

George raised the blade and plunged it into the heart of darkness. A horrible cacophony ensured, and light filled the screen. When the light cleared, he was no longer in a cave with a sword. Instead, he sat in loose pale-blue cotton clothes and rubbed his wrists while he sat in a plastic chair. His pointed ears were gone, and his head was shaved.

A man sat across from him, a notepad and pen in hand. "Tell me again about your dreams, George. They seem to constantly advance every few weeks. The last time we talked, you suggested you were about to complete your quest on this fantasy world of Oriceran. That you would slay all the evil there."

"There's a whole other world out there, Doctor Yang," the hero insisted. "It's real. Oriceran's not a lie. They've simply kept the truth from us."

"If Oriceran's real, why are you here? Why aren't you there fighting the darkness? Don't you see, George? It's a coping mechanism. You can't get over the fact that your wife died in that car accident. You blame yourself because you were texting." The therapist offered him a soft smile. "You keep blocking this out. You were looking at a text—an order for ceramics—and took your eyes off the road. They were supposed to be an anniversary gift. Ordering ceramics got converted to Oriceran in your mind. You need to face the truth."

The next ten minutes proceeded with George's anguish in what appeared to be a mental hospital in upstate New York. Even though they didn't specify the date, judging by the computers and phones, it was probably the late 2000s, maybe early 2010s, a period before the gates had started opening and the truth of magic had emerged.

"I accept it," a tearful George said in his final therapy session of the film. "I killed my wife."

"Acceptance of the truth is the first step on the road to recovery," Doctor Yang responded, a warm smile on his face. "We'll help you with the rest."

He lowered his face to his hands and sobbed.

The scene cut to Doctor Yang in his office. He reached into his desk and pulled out a wand. After he'd listened for a moment to ensure he was alone and no one approached, he waved and intoned a spell. A translucent image of a Light Elf appeared.

"Status?" the elf asked.

"He's convinced that Oriceran's a lie, a mental fabrication." Doctor Yang sighed. "I don't know why this particular man's powers made him so sensitive, even if some of the details bleeding over were incorrect. Perhaps he's meant to be a Seer, but the secret of magic and Oriceran is safe for now. You can trust in the Silver Griffins."

The movie faded to black.

Raine was the first one to speak. "Interesting. It's almost a retread of some of the stuff he's done in earlier movies, but it's still interesting."

Philip frowned. "I get what he was trying to do now with the way George talked, but I'm with Raine. I spent most of the movie confused why he sounded like that when no one around him did."

Cameron shook his head. "I don't like it. *The Sixth Sense* still works as a dramatic movie even if you know about the twist, but I feel like this is a puzzle that's not interesting when solved."

Sara rubbed her shoulders. "It freaks me out. That kind of thing happened, you know."

Madelyn's eyes widened. "It did?"

The kitsune nodded. "It happened to Headmistress Berens' daughter. She knew about Oriceran, and they locked her up."

Raine sighed. "I've heard that."

William frowned. "Were the Griffins involved like in the movie?"

Sara shrugged. "I don't know all the details, and I think it was more that normal non-magicals thought she was crazy. I know she spent years in the mental hospital and wasn't freed until shortly before the gates were opened. I think it had something to do with Leira Berens and the Fixer."

Even if the headmistress didn't play up the exploits of her granddaughter, every magical had heard of her. She was, after all, the first modern magical bounty hunter, and that was before considering her relationship with the current Fixer, Correk.

Raine shivered. "So if I'd come into my power before the gates opened, I might have been locked up somewhere?"

"Not necessarily, but it could have happened." Adrien's expression turned grim, and he nodded. "They didn't always keep the secret in the most humane of ways. They might have had their reasons, but that didn't mean all their tactics were ethical."

"Then even if this isn't the best movie on its own merits," she began, "I think it's good in that it raises an important part of history that's glossed over."

She turned back toward the television. The credits continued to scroll. How many hidden truths could there be even in an average movie?

CHAPTER TWENTY-FIVE

Agent Connor smiled at Raine as she ducked her head into his small office.

"William said you wanted to see me?" she asked. "But he said it wasn't urgent."

He gestured to the single gray folding metal chair in front of his small desk. She closed the door behind her and took a seat.

"Yes, Raine," he confirmed. "I wanted to touch base with you since we're closer to the end of the semester than the beginning."

Raine sighed. "We are, aren't we? Time flows together between classes, FBI training, and the library. It feels like only yesterday I stepped onto the campus for the first time."

The agent chuckled. "You're far too young to wax nostalgic. Wait a few decades, at least, and then it won't make me feel so old."

"Okay." Raine grinned. "I'll try. But what's this about?"

"I wanted to let you know that I've been in close

communication with the bureau about your special dispensation in case any issues arise. This situation is as much political as it is anything else, and while I'm not the greatest political warrior in the bureau, I have contacts I can draw on if things get messy."

She frowned, a little disquieted by this statement. "Are you saying there's been a problem?"

He shook his head. "They've made it clear there are no problems. To the best of my knowledge, everything is ready for you to start at the academy this September. The FBI is eager for you to join—eager enough that it wouldn't hurt if you prepared a few standard answers to interview questions about your background and that kind of thing. They definitely will want to get their PR value out of you."

With a small frown, he continued. "There are still a few details to be worked out about how to deal with your magic during training, but for now, plan to bring your wand, and if they don't want you to use magic, they'll tell you. I suspect they'll have you go magic-free for the Academy, and they'll then decide the best ways to use your magic in the field as an agent. Things are in flux, and there's already talk of modifying Hogan's Alley to better reflect magic. In addition, there's the constitutional aspect. As we've gone over during your training, there are still many legal restrictions on different types of magic, and it's important that the bureau follows all proper procedures so no cases or evidence are thrown out."

Raine nodded. He'd drilled the information into her head repeatedly. She felt like she was taking law school courses half the time. "Of course. Is that what you wanted to talk about?"

"No, I merely wanted to make that clear." Agent Connor shook his head. "It's a huge deal for you to be the first witch to openly serve in the FBI, and it's a huge deal for you to enter the bureau immediately out of high school. I've supported you in this because I believe in your dedication and potential, but given what happened with William, I also want to make sure that you're not dedicated to joining the FBI early because you believe you have to rather than because you want to. That's a good way to start your career on the wrong foot."

"I want to." She shrugged. "Nothing's changed from before. It wouldn't have changed even if I didn't have magic."

"Keep in mind, no one will hold it against you if you want to go to college first. You might not be the official first witch in the FBI in that case, but I can still guarantee your acceptance even if you delay. You've already proven your bravery and your investigatory instincts."

Raine shook her head. "No. I'm dedicated and focused on becoming an FBI agent starting this September. I don't see any reason to delay. I'm not knocking college, but part of the reason people go to school is to find themselves and learn the skills they need for their job. I already found myself here, and you've taught the basic skills I need to know. The FBI will teach me the rest. Waiting at this point would simply be a waste of everyone's time."

Agent Connor sighed. He folded his hands in front of him. "This is personal, and you might even find it intrusive, but it's important that I ask it because everyone who joins the bureau needs to do so for the right reasons. That way, we have the best agents with the best motivations."

Her stomach knotted. "I'm ready and willing for you to ask any questions you want. I'll even do it under a truth spell if you prefer."

"That's not necessary." He looked thoughtful for a second. "The bureau might be accepting of magic, but they still don't trust truth magic all that much, and nor do the courts, for the most part. Maybe you can help them change their opinion on that. I'll be very direct with you as your mentor and as a future colleague. If you're joining the FBI to solve your father's murder, don't."

She blinked. "Excuse me?"

"I understand if you want to join the FBI to find your father's killers, but it's a cold case. I don't think I've always been clear enough on that point with you." He shook his head. "And some magic has already been used to investigate it. The sad reality is that most cold cases are never solved. Even *if* the bureau allowed you to investigate the murder, you might not ever be able to solve it. I'd even go so far as to say it's unlikely you will. That's what I'm trying to be clear about." He frowned. "You should join the FBI because you want to help solve crimes and better integrate magicals into federal law enforcement. Even though your background can inspire you, it can't be your primary motivation." He pointed at her. "I know that idea's been in the back of your mind, so I thought it important to address it directly."

Raine took a deep breath and released it slowly. "Of course it has been. There's no way I could argue that it hasn't, but I also understand everything you told me. You've had me study the statistics, and you've had me read victim statements so I can better understand the effects of crime on citizens, but it doesn't matter."

Agent Connor's brow raised. "It doesn't matter?"

"There are different ways to serve my father's memory." She smiled. "I'd love to catch his killer, but if I'm a good agent and I continue to help apprehend and stop criminals and protect innocent people, I'll also be serving his memory and in a way that'll last longer and help more people. I want to make the world a better place, first and foremost. I'm not joining the bureau for revenge."

"Okay. Good. As long as we're on the same page." He extended his hand. "I know we have six months until September but let me be the first to officially welcome you into the FBI."

She gave his hand a firm shake. Cameron had a path for the future, and their commitment to their relationship remained strong. Her entrance to the FBI Academy also remained in place. The future beckoned brightly.

CHAPTER TWENTY-SIX

Adrien took a deep breath as Hilda, Carlos, Irina, and Dennis formed up behind him in a loose V formation. They had materialized in the match seconds before, and he already felt uneasy. He looked up at the glowing sign floating over the sand-covered road that cut through the massive lifeless dunes surrounding them.

FIND THE COMPASS PIECES IN THE FOUR LANDS TO POINT TO THE FINAL LOCATION OF THE TOKEN. BEWARE THE CHANGING ENVIRONMENTS AND THE FOES THEREIN.

THE ROAD WILL LEAD YOU TO WHERE YOU'LL NEED TO BE EVENTUALLY.

"It's like nested Louper," he muttered and gestured to the road. "But it doesn't seem like they want things to be that hard, to begin with." He nodded to Hilda. "See if you can track the token. It might be a trick."

The witch raised her wand and cast the tracking spell. No orb appeared, and she shook her head.

Something glinted in the sand off to the side of the

road. The elf jogged toward it and knelt. He brushed the sand away and found a fragment of a white compass, about one-eighth of the full device judging by the arc of the segment.

With a shrug, he returned and handed it to Hilda. "Let's see if they'll let us track the other end."

This time, the spell produced a tracking orb indicating that they shouldn't actually follow the road.

Adrien nodded. "We have a goal. Let's complete it."

The Cardinals traversed the vast dunes, trudging up and down the seemingly endless hills of sand as they closed on the compass piece. After ten minutes of walking, palm trees appeared in the distance—an oasis. The team continued their march toward it and expected to see their opponents in the Louper finals, the Dallas Fireflies, but there was no one there. Now ten yards away from the edge, they didn't even see any animals.

Adrien liked the idea of another complete shut-out, but the Fireflies had only gotten stronger as the season continued. Any slips up could mean that the Cardinals would fail to bring home another championship.

The sun darkened for a moment, and he looked up. "I doubt that's only for atmosphere. I think that's supposed to their version of a roc."

A massive brown-and-white bird of prey with razor-sharp talons circled overhead. While it was hard to judge its absolute size at a distance, the expanse of its shadow suggested a bird as large as a small passenger jet.

According to magical scholars, such creatures had once roamed Earth's Middle East in the distant past when the gates were opened before, but like many legendary magical beasts, they hadn't survived the closing of the gates and now only lived on as a memory.

The captain summoned a sword. "Everyone, shield up."

They immediately layered shields over themselves and raised their wands to hold them pointed at the roc. A keening cry erupted from the bird as it dove toward the oasis.

"Okay, split up," he shouted. He burst toward one of the trees. The others ran or used spell bursts until all five Cardinals were at least ten yards apart.

The monster reared in mid-flight and flapped its wings to arrest its fall. The trees swayed under the wind it created, and the water rippled. The bird screeched and banked toward Adrien.

He rolled out of the way as the massive beak snapped at him. It missed and sliced through the thick trunk of a palm tree. The top of the tree fell into the water and created enough of a splash to give the elf a shower.

Adrien stumbled in the sand, his teeth gritted. He released the energy fueling the sword and fired a small blast of light magic at the roc. It screeched and jerked back, then beat its wings even harder and churned up a flurry of sand.

"I'll keep it busy," he shouted, his arm in front of his face. "We trained for this exact scenario. Bring it down together, and I'll finish it."

"We trained to take down something big, not necessarily a giant bird," Carlos called in response.

"The same principles apply. I'll keep it low and focused on me. Hurry and get into position, but wait for the right moment." He fired another blast into the bird's chest. The strike blew a few feathers off and seared the skin beneath. He burst away as the roc divebombed him.

The combination of running, bursting, and sniping succeeded not only in keeping the mammoth-sized creature focused on the elf but to anger it as well. The flap of the massive wings constantly sprayed sand in his face. Even though his shields protected his eyes, they didn't do anything about the lack of visibility, which slowed his movements.

He glanced toward the other players through the settling dust. They stood close together, their wands pointed, and chanted. As underclassmen, their knowledge of most joint ritual magic was limited, but he'd sought permission to provide training in a Louper context. They'd been able to achieve impressive feats in practice, but accomplishing it under match pressure was a different thing entirely.

The roc lunged toward Adrien, its beak open. His teammates shouted the final words of their incantation together. A fine silver-colored mesh net materialized in front of the bird. Its momentum helped to wrap it around the target. The creature strained to free itself, but the material held.

Adrien burst to the side as the giant beast crashed and kicked up a massive cloud of sand and dust. He shook his head to clear it and summoned a sword. His adversary glared balefully at him and fought the restraints but only managed to entangle itself even further. He sprinted toward the downed bird and thrust his sword deep into its exposed neck. The roc thrashed for a few seconds and it glowed momentarily. In the next breath, it turned into sand.

Light reflected off something in the center of the pile. He jogged over to it and retrieved the compass piece. As soon as he placed it against the other one, they fused together.

"Let's get back to the road," the captain shouted. "My guess is it takes us into the next zone."

After more walking and a sudden shift from the desert to the frozen arctic, the team arrived in front of a series of stacked ice disks of ascending diameter. The smallest measured about a yard, and the largest almost three yards across. A metal pole ran through their center, and two other empty metal poles stood behind them. Their tracking clearly indicated the next compass piece was in the area, but it turned erratic once they moved closer to the discs.

Adrien grinned. "Do you see what I see?"

Irina nodded. "This is a Tower of Hanoi puzzle."

The rules were straightforward. A larger disk couldn't be placed on top of a smaller disk. Only a single disk could be moved at a time. Each move involved taking the top disk from a stack and placing it either on top of a different stack or on an empty rod. The final goal was to move the entire stack to another rod obeying those rules and in the minimum number of moves.

"We've all studied this one. Be careful and have two people use magic to move each disk. I'll call the moves out, and we'll get this done as quickly as possible."

Hilda and Dennis ferried the smallest ice disk with the help of light ropes to the second rod to set it on top of the newly formed tower. It had taken more time to move the pieces than actually determine the moves. As the final one settled into place, the entire tower glowed brightly for several seconds before it melted the water around the puzzle. The liquid receded to reveal a compass piece.

Adrien walked over to it and raised an eyebrow. He lifted it and placed it against the other fused piece, and the magic repeated itself. "It's one fourth, not one-eighth. So, we're halfway there." He pointed to the road, which continued past the puzzle. "Let's get our next piece before Dallas does."

CHAPTER TWENTY-SEVEN

The next zone passed swiftly. It was a forest infested with rabid six-legged rabbits but no puzzles, and they could make short work of most battle challenges that didn't involve massive behemoths. Once the team had finished their quick, bloodless butchery, they located the next compass piece in a mound of dirt near the monsters' lair.

To Adrien's surprise, when they traveled farther up the road, they found the last piece of the compass lying on a pedestal beside the road immediately after the zone transitioned to a rancid swamp. No clever tricks, no monsters, and no puzzles might seem like a bonus, but it unsettled him.

"I'm not the only one who gets nervous when something is too easy, right?" he asked.

The other four players shook their heads.

He snorted and slipped the last compass piece into place. It fused with a flash and the needle spun for a few seconds before it stopped and pointed deeper into the swamp. Unfortunately, the road dead-ended shortly after the pedestal.

"I suppose if you simply followed the road and found half the compass, you might feel fairly good about things," the captain said. "But I'm glad we're here now. Everyone, shield up again. We don't know what's in the swamp. That's a lot of dark water in which to hide something nasty."

The team refreshed their defenses and followed him as he waded waist-high through the mist and the vegetation-filled murky water. The greatest challenge was the smell. Some kind of super-alligator seemed the obvious possible monster threat, but there wasn't enough land for them to burst from place to place, and it'd take too much time to build a bridge with magic. Simply wading through was the most efficient way to their goal.

Adrien constantly scanned the distant trees for signs of ambush or suspicious shadows or flashes of light, but the swamp, unlike a real one, was strangely quiet and devoid of life. It lacked even the incessant insects that all but defined actual wetlands. His heart pounded in his chest. All their effort for the entire year—and all his training for four years—would come to a conclusion in the next few minutes.

"I can't believe it," Dennis said. "We're almost there. We'll take the championship and have a perfect season. We're good."

The elf smiled. Everyone obviously shared the same thoughts. That was a sign of a well-synched team, but they couldn't afford to get cocky.

He shook his head. "Only claim victory once it's actually happened. To do so before then is to lack discipline. There's another trick here yet. We simply have to find it."

"You never loosen up, do you?" the other boy grinned. "Have you seen that movie *Manic Human Dream Girl?* But then again, you do have a girlfriend, and you're still as stiff as—" He winced under his captain's withering glare.

"We don't have time to prattle about my personal life," Adrien snapped. "It's as you said. We're close to victory and I, for one, want that victory."

The team continued in silence, the only noise the slight splashing as they waded through the sludgy water and followed the compass direction. About five minutes had passed when five people appeared through the mists. The Dallas Fireflies.

Both teams halted with about fifty yards between them. The elf drew a deep breath. Perhaps if the teams hadn't been so balanced, a few super-alligators would have appeared to slow one of them down. He would never know, but he would gladly face whatever conjured monster the game might involve than the five thinking and well-trained Louper players.

"They didn't lose a single player," he muttered. "That complicates things. I assumed they faced their own roc and perhaps lost at least one person." He glanced at the compass. "But their presence here clarifies other things."

Hilda's fingers flexed around her wand. "What do you mean?"

"If they're here and we're here, and we're both using compasses, it means the token is somewhere around here. It *has* to be between us, and that means it's probably less than fifty yards away."

"Okay. But where? I've been looking, and I haven't seen anything that looks like a golden token."

"You need to think like the match designers for a final." He sighed. "What would be the most annoying place to hide the token in a swamp?"

"Underwater," everyone murmured at once.

"Exactly." He shook his head.

The Dallas players spread out in the distance and crept forward.

"It looks like they're catching on too," Adrien said. "I'll end this with speed. Let's go with a water distraction plan. It might not have involved a swamp, but we did practice this scenario. Give me the cover, and I'll bring you your victory."

Dennis whipped his wand up and shouted an incantation. Water erupted near one of the Fireflies. Hilda, Carlos, and Irina followed up with their own spells, either waves or showers of disgusting swamp water. The Fireflies launched a counterattack and soon, dark water fountained and fell continuously from the sky like tainted rain to obscure their vision and cause even wilder poorly aimed attacks.

The elf summoned an air bubble spell and wrapped a small illuminated air bubble around the compass and the front of his other hand to make it easier for him to cast while underwater. He'd learned that the hard way in previous matches. Magic required precise movements, and it was sometimes hard to achieve any level of success in water unless you were a species native to it.

He dove under the surface and looked at the compass. After a few more seconds, he kicked forward and followed with an underwater burst. The spell rocketed him forward like a torpedo. The water churned continuously around him as both teams attempted to distract one another.

The slight hope of utterly destroying the enemy team and never even having to face them had lingered at the beginning of the match with the different zones and challenges. Earlier successes only fed the idea, but now, Adrien chastised his own arrogance and his stomach roiled as hard as the water. It was too close.

He glided forward, his gaze on the compass. The needle turned abruptly, and he cast another quick burst for lateral movement. The needle swung again, and he used a final spell to counter his forward momentum and bring himself to an abrupt stop. He swam lower, raised his free hand to cast another spell, and hoped the clear words allowed by the air bubble would enable him to use the magic without too much difficulty. The match would likely be decided in the next minute, if not the next thirty seconds.

The muck and particulates in the water near the bottom separated and the light from his compass's bubble illuminated the token several yards down. It beckoned, so tantalizing close. A bright ball careened through the water and powered into him. The attack catapulted him away and his compass fell from his hand.

The captain shook his head and growled. A quick roll saved him from another blast as much as his shields had saved him from the first. The shadowy form of an opponent floated in the distance.

Adrien replied not with an attack but a hasty ice spell instead. A few chunks appeared halfway between him and the Dallas player. One of them shattered into dozens of smaller pieces a second later. He didn't wait or launch another attack but directed himself toward the token and burst downward, his hand outstretched.

Five yards. Four yards. Three yards. Two yards. Another powerful magical blast pummeled his chest. His shield failed and he groaned and pumped his legs as hard as he could.

He stretched desperately but was still too far away. While he couldn't directly manipulate the token with his magic, he didn't have to, especially in this environment. He motioned decisively in front of him with his hands and quickly chanted a spell.

The water began to swirl around the token as another blast struck him. His avatar wasn't likely to survive many more like that, but he ignored the attack and continued to stir the water. The current caught the golden disk.

The Light Elf seized his chance. He burst again as his opponent landed a third strike in his side. Thankfully, it no longer mattered. He swirled past the spinning token and snatched it with two fingers.

The marsh disappeared in an instant as the Louper gear reset. He could now see only the real world.

"The winner," declared an announcer, "of the Louper finals match between the Charlottesville Cardinals and the Dallas Fireflies is the Cardinals. Congratulations, School of Necessary Magic, on your perfect season!"

The students filling the stands shouted as a collective, their voices a thunderous exultation of victory. Adrien grinned and pulled his headset off. He walked over to shake the hands of the other team members.

"You did it," Dennis said and his eyes glistened. "You led us to victory."

The captain shook his head. "No. *We* did it. Without your effort and practice, none of this would have happened." The team charged him, including the players waiting off to the side as subs. They all tackled him in a hug as the spectators roared.

CHAPTER TWENTY-EIGHT

Raine strolled across the grounds on her way to the kemana. Cameron was busy helping Philip with a project, and she decided it wouldn't hurt to spend a little free time looking around for Thothites. Each passing day made the idea seem less useful, but she'd already completed two weeks of FBI training materials over the course of the last few days and needed a diversion.

Her thoughts drifted as she walked and after a few minutes, she noticed Erin and a few other girls crouched around a tree. They spoke in furtive whispers and gestured in the general direction of the hidden kemana entrance. Erin looked up and grimaced as she made eye contact with her. She muttered something to the other girls, and they all nodded and headed toward the kemana, wearing the kind of smug looks of confidence only freshmen could manage.

Erin sighed and jogged over to her. "Hey, Raine."

"Those are all other freshmen," she said. "And I haven't seen you around with them before."

"Yes. I decided to take your advice about not going to the kemana alone. Some are friends of friends. That kind of thing. We're all going to Bubble & Fizz and a few other places." She sighed. "But now I feel bad about it. It's not like it's a big secret or something, and I felt okay, but then I saw you and that reminded me of some stuff." She shrugged, her eyes downcast. "You know?"

"You feel bad? Why? Because of the policy?" Raine glanced over her shoulder. No one else was nearby, although that didn't mean a less tolerant professor might not appear at any moment and ask where the freshman girl was going.

"No, nothing like that. I'm sad because Madelyn still can't come." Erin at picked at her fingernail with her thumb. "I've asked her a few times if she minds because I don't want to feel like I'm neglecting her or trying to push her out, but she always says she's fine and tells me not to worry, but you know how she is. She worries about offending people, and I know I really hurt her feelings earlier in the year. I think how she feels lets me get away with too much if that makes sense. Ugh. People are hard."

"They can be, but it's a good thing you care so much about her feelings." Raine nodded. "I've also talked to her about the kemana, and she's told me the entire year that she doesn't mind. I'll admit I've been worried about her myself. I've had many of the same thoughts you have as well about guilt and it not being fair, and I've gone to the kemana within the rules for years now." She shrugged.

The girl's eyes widened. "Really? Raine Campbell, senior and leader of the FBI Trouble Squad, feels the same kind of guilt? Weird."

"Yes. It comes from the same place. We both care about her. Madelyn's an unusual girl with an even more unusual background, but that doesn't mean she's not our friend. Of course we don't want her alone or to think we don't care about her, but let me tell you a little secret I've had to come to accept myself to help her grow."

"What's that?" Erin licked her lips, her eyes wide with anticipation.

Raine smiled. "Madelyn is the kind of person who needs a few friends but not many, and she's able to do a fair amount on her own. Many of the activities she enjoys, such as reading, are rather solitary things. By the way, I see you guys in the dining hall all the time, and you seem to get along fine. She smiles and laughs all the time, and it's obvious she enjoys your company. I remember what she used to be like, and it's almost shocking. She might as well have been a different girl."

Erin sighed. "I know all that, but I sometimes wonder if it's all right for me to have this kind of separate life from her. It feels sleazy somehow."

She chuckled. "Sleazy?"

"Yes. Even though it's not like I hide it from her, I still feel like I'm betraying her." She kicked at the grass. "I'd invite her if she could come along, and I know she thinks I shouldn't go, but the only reason she doesn't go is because of that crazy cult lady who wants to drink her soul or whatever." She glared at the ground and kicked it again as if it were Cina. "I'm sure if it wasn't for her, Madelyn would hang out with me more." She waved her hands in front of her. "But I'm not trying to replace her. I promise. I only want to go to the kemana every now and again, and I think the best way to do it is with other people."

"Of course. It's not wrong to have different circles of friends."

Erin scoffed. "You say that, but the FBI Trouble Squad is famous around here. You guys are super-tight friends."

"Sure, but that doesn't mean we don't have any other friends." Raine placed her hand over her heart. "My closest friends mean a lot to me, but they're not my only friends. Madelyn comes to our movie nights, even if she doesn't hang out with us much otherwise. Adrien has spent tons of time with the Louper team not only this year but throughout his entire time here. Evie used to live in the kitchens with the pixies, and the only reason she's not been there as much this year is because she's done extra-curricular potions work with Professor Fowler. Philip belongs to the Entrepreneurs' Club, and Sara the Art Club." She shrugged. "Every single one of my friends has separate circles of acquaintances and friends. Sure, it's a small school, and we all know one another, but I'm sure the artists Sara spends time around are closer to her than they are to me. I used to be Student Council and felt a kinship with many people there that I don't have with the current Student Council."

"Huh." Erin sighed. "I'm kind of shy, so I haven't done much with clubs yet. I guess that's why it's weird for me. I didn't really have much in the way of friends before Madelyn, but somehow, after hanging out with her, I felt more confident and I started hanging out with other people." She shook her head. "And that's what I'm worried about. I want to make sure I'm not treating her as a starter friend and leaving her behind."

Raine released a wistful sigh. "Let me give you a little senior advice. It's hard to go through life without making some connections that you might not later have to revisit, but for now, don't worry about it so much. Find the people you enjoy spending time with and spend time with them, even if you have to split your days up. No single friend should have a monopoly on you as a person. Madelyn understands that, and the only reason she interfered with your plans before was because of safety."

"I get that." The girl's shoulders slumped. "I wish it could be different."

"We all do." She glanced at the other girls receding in the distance. "One thing I will say—and I know this is somewhat hypocritical—but you need to be careful about going into the kemana too much as a freshman. I understand that it's not that long until summer, but keep in mind that the professors can choose to look the other way, but that doesn't mean they *have* to look the other way."

"Understood." Erin nodded quickly and gestured toward her friends. "Thanks, Raine. You've helped me feel better about things, and you're right. I spend a lot of time with Madelyn, and I shouldn't feel bad because I don't spend all my time with her. You've given me a lot to think about." She waved and jogged after the others.

Raine watched until she caught up. The cycle started over anew. Such was the fate of any school. Different personalities came together and learned to be friends or even enemies. She shook her head and turned toward the main mansion, no longer interested in visiting the kemana herself.

May's arrival meant time was running out for anyone to find Cina before Raine's graduation. The thought depressed her, but she tried to remind herself that she was a student and there wasn't anything she could do to help Madelyn other than what she had done before. Sometimes, not every loose thread in life was neatly tied up.

CHAPTER TWENTY-NINE

A few days later, Raine bit into a piece of halibut when Philip laughed for no apparent reason. She set her fork down and eyed him curiously. Everybody had concentrated on their meals, so she had no idea what he found so amusing.

Sara looked at him. "You're my favorite boy, but have you suddenly lost it because of some weird invention at the Entrepreneurs' club? If so, I'll need to find a cure."

He shook his head. "No, but...it's almost here. Graduation." He made jazz hands. "It's not months away now. It's weeks away. We're all seniors, and we'll be leaving. It's struck me in a way it hasn't before." He grinned at Adrien. "And some of us are leaving as champions."

The elf shrugged with a slight smirk.

The kitsune frowned and picked her fork up. "So? It's not like graduation is some huge surprise. It's only been coming for four years."

Philip sighed. "No, but we've had a normal semester for once. We've all been busy and focused on classes with no crazy ferrets or Willen and no chaos witches. I'm reminded of the start of my time at the school when we were still getting to know each other and trying to work everything out. Sure, Raine messed around with the druids, but we were simply kids going to school and finding ourselves. Now, we're the FBI Trouble Squad, the kind of people who confront chaos witches and the Raven Clan. That's something special, and I won't get weepy or anything, but it's something we'll never have again. We'll keep in touch and visit each other, but we're all going our separate ways and it won't be the same." He nodded at Raine. "I want to take this opportunity to say thank you for all that."

She shrugged.

Cameron frowned. "Thank you?"

"Yeah, thank you, dude. Why wouldn't I say that to Raine?" The wizard shook his head. "I wasn't the best person when I started here. I accept that. Some of the stunts I pulled made me deserve a punch in the face." He shrugged. "I was far too obsessed with money, and I made poor choices, but I've thought about this. Raine's kind of the heart of our group. We all have our individuality and our different personalities, but she's the one who brought us all together." He smiled at Sara. "And because I was involved in this group, not only have I learned to use my powers in a better way, but I also ended up dating you, and you're way better than money."

The kitsune arched her brows and smirked. "Shouldn't you thank me, then, and not Raine?"

He laughed. "I thank you all the time for being awesome, and I love you, but Raine being here helped set me up to meet you, so I'm grateful."

Sara looked at her plate, her cheeks scarlet. "I understand. Of course Raine rocks. You were all there for me during the trouble with my parents, but she was at the heart of it. She had to struggle to understand this entire new world and she still found time to help me out because of my stupid family issues."

Cameron offered his girlfriend a lop-sided grin. "You know I love you, and you know I think you're great. I don't have much more to say."

Adrien nodded. "I say this as a Guardian—you're an honor to fight beside, Raine."

"A necessary witch," William murmured. They all glanced at him and he shrugged. "If this is the School of Necessary Magic, then Raine's the necessary witch who made our group possible. She is the heart of the FBI Trouble Squad. She's even why we're called an FBI squad, even if I'm now joining too. I hope to work with her someday in the bureau." He released a contented sigh and blinked a few times as if trying to stifle tears. "I'll miss this place more than I realized."

"We all will," Evie said and patted his shoulder. "But we'll always have all our memories."

Raine couldn't do anything but smile at her friends. "I'm honored that you all feel that way, but you're as necessary to me. I came to this school ignorant about magic and had no clue what the future would bring, and you all helped me believe in myself. I couldn't have asked for a better group of friends."

Philip raised his glass of water. "To the FBI Trouble Squad."

They all raised their juices, waters, and sodas. "To the FBI Trouble Squad."

Several other students turned toward them, confused looks on their faces. The Trouble Squad laughed.

Raine strolled back to the hallway leading to the grand stairs. Erin crept toward her but her every movement screamed suspicious. Given how guilty the girl looked most of the time, it was amazing she hadn't been caught and punished by a professor.

She froze as the senior passed her.

Fighting back her laughter, she stopped to look at the girl. "You do realize that I can see you, right? If someone gave you a fake potion, I'm sorry."

Erin grimaced. "Sorry, I guess I panicked." She swallowed and leaned forward. "I'm taking a quick trip to the kemana," she whispered. "It made me nervous since it's close to curfew, but I know you won't rat me out."

"I don't think that's a good idea." She frowned. "It's not like I don't think you should go at all, but you just gave me a good reason why you shouldn't. It's late. What could be so important that you have to go to the kemana at this very moment?"

"It's a gift for Madelyn. It's this perfect broach I saw for her earlier. I should have bought it when I was there before, but I hesitated, and other people were looking at it." Erin nodded, determination on her face. "If I don't go right away, it won't be there."

"And you're what? Simply going to duck out to the kemana alone?"

The girl hesitated and slowly shook her head. "Nothing like that. I have one other girl who will go with me. It's no big deal and it'll be a quick trip. I need this, Raine." She took a deep breath and nodded. "I need to do something nice for Madelyn. It's not like I'm sneaking into the kemana to fight crime or anything. It won't be a big deal." She waved and rushed off before she could respond.

Raine considered turning her in to a professor, but the sheer hypocrisy of the act galled her. Erin simply wanted to buy a present for a friend and wasn't risking her life, unlike many of the times she and her friends had violated kemana restrictions.

Every freshman had to learn their place at the school. If Erin got caught and in trouble, she would do so having known the risks.

She shook her head. It was hard to grow up. Now, she often related more to Headmistress Berens and her stress than a freshman girl who wanted to buy a pretty present for a friend.

CHAPTER THIRTY

A huge yawn caught Raine unawares as she stepped outside the library. With graduation so close, she couldn't resist the temptation to spend a few extra hours there. She doubted the FBI had a magical library as impressive, and she also doubted she would ever again have a time in her life when she would have the freedom to spend so much time reading books of general interest. Helping to stock a decent magical FBI library would give her a good reason to keep in contact with Head Librarian Decker, along with providing her with a way to channel her love of books into synergy with her upcoming career as an FBI agent.

Agents Connor and Oliver rushed down the hallway toward her and both looked worried. She stopped and waited for them.

The PDA agent frowned. "There you are. We've been looking for you. Your roommates said you were here and I'm glad they were right. The last thing we need is more trouble."

"Is there a problem?" she asked. "What's going on?"

She hadn't felt anything unusual magically in the library, and the gnomes hadn't acted concerned. That suggested the school wasn't under attack or being invaded by a chaos witch.

The agents exchanged glances. Agent Connor nodded to his counterpart.

The woman drew a deep breath. "You wouldn't happen to know where Erin or Madelyn are, would you? Even if you've promised not to tell on them, you need to be honest right now."

"Madelyn?" Raine shook her head. "No, I haven't seen her since from across the room at dinner." She sighed. While she didn't want to tell them where Erin was, she couldn't lie to two federal agents, including her mentor. "I think I might know where Erin is."

Agent Oliver nodded up the hall. "Come with us. We need to talk to the headmistress." She stepped away without another word.

Agent Connor moved to follow her.

Raine blinked and jogged after them. "I don't understand. What's wrong?"

"Both Erin and Madelyn are missing," he said.

She gasped.

Headmistress Berens, Professor Powell, and the two agents crowded into her office a few minutes later. Raine stood rigidly in front of the desk, her hands clasped behind her back.

"The kemana?" the headmistress echoed after her brief explanation. "You're sure?"

She nodded. "She said she was going there with someone else to pick something up—a present for Madelyn."

Instinctively, she tensed, waiting to be berated for allowing the girl to leave.

Instead, the woman sighed. "If she said she was leaving with someone else, that might explain where Madelyn is. No other student is unaccounted for. Has Madelyn ever mentioned leaving the school grounds to you, Raine? Please be honest. You, of all students, understand the stakes here and the risk."

Raine shook her head. "No, she's been very clear that she doesn't want to leave while Cina's out there. She even fought with Erin earlier this semester about going into the kemana. Erin has done the standard freshman sneak off to the kemana, but there's no way Madelyn has. It makes no sense. She doesn't like the kemana all that much, and if she intended to go, she's skittish enough that I'm sure she would ask for my help."

"I don't know why we bother with the rule given that every student seems to think it's a mere suggestion." Headmistress Berens looked at Professor Powell. "What do you think?"

He shrugged. "We all tried our tracking spells and they didn't work. I don't know. They probably have to be together for this to make sense. Madelyn must be blocking the tracking somehow. We all know her magical power level and ability isn't always consistent with her young Coral Elf artificial body. There's no way Erin has the skill necessary to block us, so it only makes sense that they're together."

Raine's heart rate kicked up. "It makes no sense for her to leave. She's not...like many of the students. She's afraid of angering you all, and she wouldn't willingly ignore the risk and the direct request to avoid the kemana for her safety."

Agent Oliver pushed her glasses up. "Be that as it may, Raine. It doesn't change the fact that they are both gone, and the only logical conclusion is that they are together."

Agent Connor folded his arms. "It might be something less sinister than any of us are imagining. It might be that Erin stayed out too late and Madelyn simply went to go get her so she wouldn't get in trouble."

She shook her head. "If that were the case, she would have come to me and asked for help." Worry pushed through and she trembled but took a deep breath and tried to control it. "I'd like to get my friends and help you lead a search in the kemana."

"What?" He frowned. "You want more students to go in there after hours?"

"We know several places Madelyn might have gone—either places we've taken her to last semester or told her about. If it isn't simply some curfew violation..." Her voice cracked. "If Cina is waiting for her, she's vulnerable. We don't have enough time to sit around and discuss the risks. I'm not saying send us in alone. I'm saying send us in with the PDA and some professors. We'll lead people where they need to go and confirm if she's there or not. It's a simple process of elimination."

Headmistress Berens frowned. "The Thothites might be involved."

"Then that's all the more reason to hurry. Every second we spend discussing this is another second that woman has to grab Madelyn."

Agent Connor cleared his throat and turned toward the headmistress. "I can continue to coordinate a search on campus. If you can't track her, it's not impossible that she's still here, but I think Raine's right. This is a time-sensitive search and we should use all the resources we have available."

She looked at Professor Powell, who nodded curtly. Agent Oliver mirrored his agreement with a grim expression.

"Very well, then," the headmistress said. "I'll send Leo to the Ruby Falls police, so they can help with a sweep. If it turns out to simply be a curfew violation, we can laugh as we figure out a way to punish the students. But for now, let's do our best to find them before someone else does."

CHAPTER THIRTY-ONE

Raine jogged through the sparse streets of Ruby Falls, Agent Oliver and Cameron right behind her, and managed to avoid a drunk Kilomea who stumbled out of an inn. Even though Ruby Falls lacked a true day-night cycle, most people still operated under similar daily rhythms to those on the surface.

Headmistress Berens and the agents had taken Raine's suggestion and formed three search teams, including Raine's team. Professor Powell, Adrien, and William worked together and were on their way to Bubble & Fizz first. Headmistress Berens, Agent Clemson, Sara, Evie, and Philip were the last group and currently headed toward a hidden bookshop. The PDA agents had already set up a quick communication spell with the help of a few previously prepared artifact crystals. They could activate the spell if any of the teams found something.

She turned a corner and her gaze darted around the area in search of the two girls. Her behavior drew a few frowns and curious looks from kemana residents, but she ignored them, desperate for any clue that might lead to Madelyn. She didn't care if everyone thought she was insane when she next returned as long she found the girl.

"We're almost there," she said and increased her pace. "It's only a few more blocks."

Agent Oliver pushed forward to match her. "And where are we going exactly?"

"The Golden Tincture," Raine said. "It's a potions shop. I raved about it to Madelyn a few weeks ago because their prices were so cheap and sometimes, you simply want to buy a potion rather than spend two weeks brewing one. I stressed to her how once she's free to come to the kemana, she might want to have a look because there are some potions that can help with concentration. That's obviously good when you want to do a lot of reading and it's late at night. Simple memory potions, that kind of thing."

Cameron grunted. "It's a long shot. I doubt she would sneak off campus to buy concentration juice."

"We'll sweep through the list as a team." She shrugged. "That's why we have the three groups. The more places we know she's not, the better chance we have of working out where she actually is."

"Head Librarian Decker should already be speaking with the Ruby Falls authorities," the agent said. "If we can't find Madelyn, they'll be able to provide additional manpower."

Raine's heart thundered. "By then, Cina will have portaled herself to Japan." She pointed to a metal sign near the street that read *The Golden Tincture*.

The trio ran toward the small, narrow shop and stopped abruptly. A closed sign hung in the window.

She rushed over and knocked loudly on the door. "Hello? Is anyone there? We need to talk to you." She banged insistently and her breaths turned ragged. Movement inside stirred her hope. Maybe Madelyn had stayed after hours in the shop to request something special.

The door opened to reveal a gnarled and annoyed-looking witch in a floppy, rumpled, wide-brimmed hat. "Do you not know how to read? We're closed."

Agent Oliver stepped forward and displayed her badge. "Liana Oliver, Paranormal Defense Agency."

The witch's eyes widened. "I haven't done anything wrong. All my import paperwork is in order, I can assure you."

The agent snorted. "I don't care about that. All I care about is if you've seen a young Coral Elf girl today."

"Coral Elf?" She frowned. "They might be memorable enough around here, but I haven't seen one of them in months. There used to be two of them wandering around—sisters, I think, and then I saw only one on occasion, but it's been a long time. I can't say I remember seeing one of them this year."

"Thank you for your time, ma'am. We apologize for any inconvenience."

The witch nodded slowly and scowled at the girl before she slammed the door closed.

She gritted her teeth and cursed. "I knew it wouldn't be that easy, but it's still frustrating."

Cameron squeezed her shoulder. "We'll find her."

Agent Oliver nodded. "Nothing from the other teams yet."

Raine stepped away from the shop and toward the

street. She froze as a whisper reached her ear. The words were unintelligible, but the voice was unmistakably Madelyn's. She threw her hand up.

Her companions halted and waited for her to explain.

She tilted her head in concentration and tried to make the voice out. This tone was clear and pleading, but the words remained distant, garbled, and distorted.

"What's going on, Raine?" Agent Oliver asked. "Do you see something?"

"I can hear Madelyn's voice. It's like she's whispering into my ear from a distance." She shook her head. "But I can't understand it."

The agent frowned and pulled her wand out. She made several sharp, precise movements as she murmured a spell. Her frown deepened. "There's definitely some unusual magic around you, but I can't trace it to the source. Something's blocking me."

Raine took a deep breath. "If I can hear her, that means she's still alive." She took a few steps down the street. The voice sounded slightly louder, but she still couldn't make anything out.

Agent Oliver tapped a glyph on her arm. "This is Oliver. We might have a lead. Stand by."

The whispers remained distant and distorted, but one word finally leaked through.

"*Help.*"

She sprinted down the street. If it could only be a little louder, maybe she could understand more then. Her companions raced after her.

"Raine!" Cameron shouted. "Wait for us."

"I can tune this somehow," she shouted in response. "There has to be a way."

Vianna had already given her life to protect her sister. There was no way she would allow that sacrifice to be in vain.

CHAPTER THIRTY-TWO

Cameron and Agent Oliver continued to call after Raine as she sprinted down the street but she ignored them. The volume of Madelyn's whispers increased with each step, however subtly. She didn't pay attention to where she ran, concerned only with the desperate need to improve the quality of the message. Madelyn was alive, and they could save her. They simply had to find her first. The girl's words might be the only clues that would help them.

Her headlong race finally ended at a massive rock wall that prevented any further progress. She gritted her teeth, ignored her burning lungs, and focused on the message.

Cameron bounded in front of her in wolf form. She'd not paid him any attention, so she had no idea when he'd shifted.

A huffing Agent Oliver appeared thirty seconds later. "We're supposed to do this as a team, Raine."

She tilted her head. "It's louder now. Madelyn's voice. Maybe I'm closer."

The shifter growled and sniffed along the wall. He shook his head after a few seconds and she took that to mean he hadn't found any real scents.

The agent frowned and wiped the sweat off her forehead. "We can't go off half-cocked on this. We need decent intelligence or eyewitness statements that tell us where the girl is."

Raine closed her eyes to concentrate on the words. "It's louder now, but it's still hard to make out. Portal. Help. Raine. I'm reasonably sure that's the core of it, but it's too hard to make anything else out." She opened her eyes. "I don't understand."

"I have an idea," the woman said. "But we'll need the other teams." She tapped her glyph. "I'll send a flare up. I need all teams to converge on my location."

Raine paced restlessly and her heart thundered as Madelyn's worried whispers repeated within her. The tense seconds seemed to stretch into hours rather than minutes before the other team arrived, along with a half-dozen Ruby Falls police officers and Head Librarian Decker.

"Portal, help, Raine," Agent Oliver said with a shrug. "That's all Raine can make out, but I think it's all we need. The message apparently grew louder as she moved, but—" She motioned to the wall. "We have nowhere else to go."

Agent Clemson frowned. "What makes you think that's all we need?"

The woman pointed at Raine. "I know the entire history of Madelyn and Vianna, remember? Raine's not merely a friend of Madelyn. She's someone Maeve wanted before she became two people. Don't ask me to explain it because I don't know the fine mechanics in this situation, but we've all dealt with and taken advantage of the power of extreme emotional resonance and personal connections in spells. I believe Madelyn is providing some kind of beacon because of her strong personal connection to Raine."

"What good does it do?" her colleague asked with a shrug. "If we can't track her directly, how will it help?"

"Because this is an emotional link between two distinct living beings," she replied. "That has to mean something."

Headmistress Berens nodded, her arms folded. "The mere fact that she can reach Raine is proof enough of that."

"We've done this kind of thing before," Professor Powell said.

The poppy on Librarian Decker's bowler hat growled. The gnome looked thoughtful. "Agent Oliver's right, as is Professor Powell. Direct tracking or even indirect tracking might be destined to fail, but if we perform a joint ritual, we might be able to force a portal open to wherever Madelyn is. She must be close if Raine can hear her. We can use her as a kind of inverted beacon to force a connection to wherever Madelyn is, and given what's going on, it's likely Erin is near as well."

One of the Ruby Falls police stepped forward and shook his head. "We're willing to help find missing students, but unless you can guarantee they're still in the kemana, this is outside our jurisdiction. Also, we can't risk leaving the area undermanned in case the Thothites come back. No offense, but everything Mr. Decker told us suggests this might be related to the cult."

The head librarian nodded. "Headmistress Berens, two trained PDA agents, myself, and Professor Powell. That should be enough unless she's in some strange pocket dimension."

Raine pointed to Cameron and gestured toward her other friends. "If the police aren't coming, you'll need all the help you can get."

Headmistress Berens frowned. "This isn't some fun little adventure, Raine. This involves a dangerous cult that thinks nothing of harming children."

"I know. I've fought them before." She snorted. "I'll be eighteen by the time I join the FBI, and that's less than six months from now. If I'm good enough to be a federal agent by then, I'm good enough to help rescue my friend now."

Cameron growled and nodded, still in wolf form.

Sara shook her head. "What's the point of Professor Powell's classes if we can't use them to help rescue one of our friends?"

The professor grinned. "She does make a persuasive argument."

Adrien slapped a hand over his chest. "I'll participate in Guardian duties when I return to France. This is my duty now."

William raised a fist. "I can't graduate in good conscience if something happens to Madelyn and I could have done something to stop it."

Philip shrugged. "And here I thought we would make it through the semester without trouble."

Evie pointed to several pouches hanging from her belt. "I didn't bring these for show."

Head Librarian Decker nodded. "We have many things and much talent among us—many resources, Mara. Time isn't one of those. Let's open the portal, let's bring the Trouble Squad, and let's save that girl."

Agent Oliver adjusted her tie. "Raine's right. Under normal circumstances, I would balk at this, but these aren't normal circumstances. This isn't only a matter of saving the girl. If the Thothites need her for a ritual and have her, something extremely dangerous might be in progress. Serious threats to kemanas aren't exactly unprecedented with recent history and fringe groups."

Headmistress Berens sighed. "Very well, then." She walked over to Raine and placed a hand on her shoulder. "This might be uncomfortable."

Raine shook head. "Do what you need to as long as it helps us save Madelyn."

The woman nodded to Head Librarian Decker. Professor Powell, the two PDA agents, and the headmistress all surrounded Raine in a rough circle, although the headmistress kept her hand on the girl's shoulder. Professor Powell and the agents pulled their wands out and began to chant. The head librarian half-closed his eyes and murmured a chant under his breath. His hands traced glyph shapes from what Raine could tell.

Warmth suffused her body, and a soft glow surrounded her. She took a few deep breaths as the warmth turned uncomfortably hot. The older magicals continued their ritual and their chants overlapped.

The light blinded her now, and her skin felt like it was

on fire. She concentrated on Madelyn's whispers. They had to save her. There was no one else who could. The glaring light vanished, and a swirling portal appeared a few yards away.

Headmistress Berens took a few deep breaths. Her face was bathed in sweat. "It won't be pinpoint accurate, but it should be close."

Raine pulled her wand out. "Time to rescue a friend."

CHAPTER THIRTY-THREE

They arrived in the middle of a sparse forest. Nothing appeared unusual about the trees. They looked very similar to those in the forests around the school, as did many of the flowers. Raine was the last one to step through the portal and she didn't need to be a botanist to guess they were probably still in Virginia at least.

"Where are we?" Agent Clemson asked as he looked around. "We could be anywhere."

"Not anywhere." Agent Oliver frowned and pulled her phone out. "We already established that this was most likely short-ranged."

"What are you doing?" He frowned. "We don't have time to call for reinforcements."

She gave him a cool look. "I'm taking advantage of technology and using a map app." She narrowed her eyes. "We're not even that far from where we were. We're in the Charlottesville area in the northeast—Maple Ridge, according to the map. From the looks of things, we could have driven here without taking too long if we knew where to drive."

Headmistress Berens glanced around. "Maple Ridge? There aren't exactly a huge number of homes in the area, nor is it a deep forest. We'll need to be cautious." She pointed to a bright light in the distance. Massive waves of magical energy flowed from it and prickled the skin of most of those present. "But it looks like we ended up close enough to whatever's going on."

Raine grimaced. "Cina's already started."

"We still don't know it's the Thothites. This might be something else entirely." The headmistress didn't sound convinced.

"It doesn't matter who it is," Agent Oliver said. "They've kidnapped a girl, and we'll stop them."

Agent Clemson nodded firmly.

The Trouble Squad began shielding themselves even before the professors and PDA agents. Evie adjusted the positions of her potions, and Sara rearranged her various seeds, berries, and other items. After a minute or so, everyone was ready, whether they relied on wands or not. The only person without a direct shield was Cameron.

Agent Oliver took a few steps toward the light. "Let's take this carefully and slowly. We don't know what we'll find over there, but we also don't have much time whatever the case."

The make-shift task force crept through the woods toward the light. Dried foliage on the forest floor crackled beneath their shoes even though they tried to advance as quietly as they could. It only took half a minute to realize the light was coming from a clearing. They pressed forward cautiously and the trees grew sparser. Finally, they slowed as they reached the edge of the open space.

Raine managed not to gasp. Madelyn hung in the air in the center, her eyes closed. Intricate glyphs of bright light covered the entire area and streams of energy juddered and flowed from the ground and into the girl. Erin lay on the edge of the clearing on the other side. She had been bound and lay on her side.

It was hard to tell if she was breathing at a distance, but it would be pointless to tie a corpse up. The girl's presence also confirmed that a faint worry of Raine's had been misplaced. She'd briefly entertained the idea that Erin had somehow been a Thothite spy, but it appeared she was merely another victim of the cult and their evil.

"Cina," she whispered.

The Thothite priestess stood in front of the Coral Elf in a bright white robe. She chanted, her arms outstretched. Her hands and pendant glowed as brightly as the glyphs. Two dozen of her followers stood in a semi-circle around her and chanted in unison. Fortunately, all their backs were turned to the rescue force.

Raine dragged in a deep breath and managed to resist the urge to charge out and demand Madelyn's release. At least this time, the Trouble Squad had backup.

CHAPTER THIRTY-FOUR

Some of her initial anger faded as Raine blew out a breath and shook out her free hand. She needed to focus on the most important aspect of the situation. Both Madelyn and Erin were still alive. They weren't too late. Everything had been heart-pounding and stomach-churning, but this didn't have to end with another death. Cina had to understand that.

Agent Oliver took a deep breath. "Let's try to give them their chance. Everyone, get ready. If we simply fling magic, we might hurt the girls."

The gathered rescue force nodded at her with the exception of Cameron, who growled.

She stepped into the clearing. "I'm Agent Liana Oliver of the Paranormal Defense Agency. We've been looking for you, Cina."

The priestess turned her head and narrowed her eyes. "Interlopers. I should have known. On the cusp our great victory, the small-minded swarm like moths to the flame that will destroy them. It is unfortunate but perhaps inevitable."

Raine stood beside the agent. The other adults moved forward, their wands or hands pointed, and the Trouble Squad students spread out on the flanks.

"This doesn't have to end poorly, Cina," Agent Oliver shouted. "If you surrender right now, I can make sure your cooperation is duly noted and it'll help with your sentencing. If you resist, I can't guarantee either your safety or that of your followers. I really don't want to hurt you."

The other Thothites turned, their faces hidden by their hoods, but their wands were raised.

The priestess scoffed. "Give up now? We have waited over a millennium for this. Our patience will be rewarded. It's too late for you to stop us now, and with the help of one of the Keys of Maat, we'll be able to unlock the power we deserve and need."

Headmistress Berens narrowed her eyes. "I can't stand by and let you hurt my students. That girl is my responsibility. I don't care about your professed aims. If they involve sacrificing a girl, they are twisted and wrong, and I won't allow it."

Professor Powell nodded. "I'm tired of hearing people like you rant and rave about how you'll change the world by sacrificing others. It always comes down to the same thing—hurting people for more power. It doesn't matter how you dress it up and what excuses you use. It's pathetic and self-serving."

Cina frowned. "You're all small-minded simpletons, comfortable in your webs of lies and what you believe about magic. You'll thank us in the end for what we're about to do, even if there are a few minor sacrifices along the way." She cut through the air with her hand. "Such is progress."

Agent Oliver shook her head. "You think I can allow this? You think I *will* allow this? I'm a PDA agent."

"I don't care what your precious laws say. They oppressed us in the past and we'll wash them away with our own power. You're nothing before the truth of what reality is—the primordial magic we'll gain access to."

Raine frowned. Cina obviously wanted to win them over ideologically. The longer they stalled whatever she was doing, the better it was for Madelyn. Besides, the priestess' actual plan remained unclear. Maybe there was some way to free the girl and convince the Thothites she wasn't necessary.

"How exactly?" she called.

Agent Oliver shot her a dirty look but didn't say anything.

"How what?" Cina asked.

Raine gestured to the floating Madelyn. "I don't understand how doing magic with Madelyn is supposed to achieve the primordial magic you've told me about. I won't pretend she's not special, but she's not a goddess. She's merely a girl."

The woman smiled, the expression almost feral. "It's as you say. She's special. I can feel it in the magic, but more to the point, she resonates with the kemana in a very specific way. It's as if she's directly linked to it."

Headmistress Berens frowned. "It might be a byproduct of how she came into existence, I suppose, but that doesn't justify anything you've said."

"You see?" Cina sneered. "You think I haven't heard the rumors about the girls born out of nothing? I will use her as a key to unlock the power of the kemana directly, and then I shall use that power to crack the barriers to the true primordial power. I will free myself of the tyranny of the gates."

Raine shook her head. "This is all merely assumption on your part. You keep talking about a power you don't even have, but you've used your talk of it to recruit people." She gestured to the pendant. "The headmistress already realized that you're simply using an artifact. If this primordial power was real, why do you need to lie to people? Do your followers know that you're lying? There's no record of the power you keep talking about—no evidence at all. You can't sacrifice someone for something that doesn't even exist."

The priestess' face contorted in a mask of utter hatred. "You stupid, arrogant little girl. You think you understand about the truths of this world because these lackwit, myopic fools have fed you propaganda at that school? You're no better than the foolish people who believed magic was never real."

Head Librarian Decker raised his hand. "Excuse me. If Madelyn is linked to the kemana, what happens to the kemana in this plan of yours?"

Cina raised her chin and squared her shoulders. "All great revolutions involve sacrifice. Such is necessary to make this world a better, stronger place."

"In other words, you'll destroy the kemana and the people in it?"

"Necessary sacrifices." She pointed at the gnome. "I've

been impressed with the strength of will of your students, and even though you fill their heads with lies, that speaks somewhat well of you. If you all swear to serve me right now and allow me to bind your will magically, I'll guarantee your survival. Otherwise, you can perish with all the sacrifices in Ruby Falls and Charlottesville."

The students gasped. The adults all glared at Cina, with the exception of Librarian Decker. He shook his head.

"You're completely insane," Agent Oliver protested. "You're talking tens of thousands of people. Even if we were to buy into your theory that some sacrifices are worth it, that's hardly a *minor* sacrifice. That's mass murder."

Agent Clemson paled.

Some of the hatred bled off Cina's face to be replaced by pity. "You have to understand that I'm not doing this because I enjoy it. I need a powerful source of magic to fuel the ritual. Unfortunately, most are near people and none of the others out there are linked to a key like the girl. Don't you understand? This is prophecy. This was foretold."

"Do you really think we'll allow you to destroy two cities for some sick experiment?" Agent Oliver asked. She raised her wand. "The only reason I haven't cut you down is because I'm trying to save lives here."

Their adversary shook her head. "I've already absorbed some of the power and shared it with my followers. You have only two choices. Join me or die."

"I order you to surrender or lethal force may be applied," the agent shouted.

"Kill all the interlopers," Cina ordered. "We've given them their chance."

CHAPTER THIRTY-FIVE

The Thothites spread out but Cina sank back and cocooned herself in a pulsating energy shield, her arms folded over her chest. Raine fired a quick light magic bolt at her, but the priestess' defenses held firm.

Her face tight with concentration, Headmistress Berens spread her arms out and a shimmering field of blue energy spread in front of the students and adults in time to absorb several explosive blue-white orbs from the cultists.

Agent Oliver fired a stun bolt at one of the cultists but his opponent's shield absorbed it. Raine followed up with a stun bolt of her own and the man stumbled. The PDA agent smiled and fired another one in tandem with the student. This time, the man dropped to his knees and twitched.

Professor Powell flourished his wand and smoothly chanted a spell. A kaleidoscopic sphere hurtled toward the enemy in a bright flash, the light mostly concentrated in one direction, a trick Raine didn't know how to achieve. Several of the Thothites reeled, their hands to their faces.

Those not blinded retreated slightly and frowned. Blocks of soil erupted from the ground. The glyphs traced over them and formed makeshift shields for many of the cultists.

"Amateurs," he muttered.

Following his professor's lead and perhaps inspired by the final big plays in the Louper final, Adrien didn't summon a sword. Instead, he focused his attacks to blow apart the dirt that protected their adversaries.

Head Librarian Decker thrust his hand out. Multiple chains appeared and wound around the blinded cultists. Agent Clemson scattered several of the others with a few quick fireballs, and William joined him. The pair continued their onslaught as if they worked together all the time in pyrokinetic cult-busting. They alternated fire to keep several of the enemy pinned down.

Cameron sprinted along the edge of the clearing and growled loudly. He drew the attention of a few of the enemy, who spun and tried to disable him with quick magical bolts but missed.

Sara hurled several acorns in high arcs behind the enemy line. They burrowed into the earth and became a quickly growing mass of woody tendrils that snarled and ripped wands from several surprised opponents. This made them easy targets for Philip, who pointed his wand and chain-fired stun bolts as quickly as he could spout the incantation.

Evie threw four vials so quickly that an observer might have thought she had used a machine or a spell. The receptacles struck several of the earthen shields and the dirt collapsed in a loose, moist pile and exposed those huddled behind them. The cultists backed away quickly, confused by what had happened.

Adrien, Philip, Raine, Agent Oliver, Agent Clemson, and Professor Powell took the opening and felled the enemy with volleys of stun bolts that overwhelmed their shields.

Cameron broke from the edge of the clearing toward the cultists. He leapt onto one, snarling and biting. His jaw locked around the wand and yanked it out of the man's hand. He snapped the wand and spun away. Some of the others turned toward the marauder wolf, which only exposed them to crossfire from the rescue force. He bounded away with a series of victorious howls.

The enemy fired ice lances, fireballs, acid, chains, and burning branches in a desperate attempt to defeat the rescue squad, but no matter what spell they tried, Headmistress Berens's defenses stopped it. Her earlier concentration had faded into a look of almost serene detachment.

"I won't allow you to harm my students," she said.

Cultist after cultist fell, either stunned, tangled in branches, or too wounded to fight. Their groans and cries fed a growing cacophony of defeat. Only a few minutes after the battle started, every enemy lay on the ground, incapacitated or unconscious, with the exception of Cina who remained snug in her shield, her eyes closed and her lips barely moving.

The students, agents, and professors all concentrated their fire—a mixture of fireballs, stun bolts, and light bolts—but the witch's shield held firm. Cameron rushed back to his allies.

The priestess opened her eyes and disappointment

filled them. "You're more resourceful than I would have anticipated, but it doesn't matter. Those men were simply more sacrifices. The battle gave me the time I needed to draw more of the kemana's power."

Professor Powell snorted. He stepped back and began chanting a spell Raine didn't recognize. His wand movements were intricate and precise and conducted so quickly, she couldn't even follow them. Sapphire light swirled around the wand.

Despite burns, cracks, holes, and unconscious men now littering the clearing, the glowing glyphs remained. The same lines of energy still flowed into Madelyn, even if they passed through cracks. The girl's eyes finally flickered open. She stared at Raine, her eyes pleading. She mouthed something, but she couldn't hear it—not even a whisper this time.

"Let Madelyn go!" she shouted. "You've lost. Just because you have a shield doesn't mean we can't get through it. You're hiding because you know you can't win. Don't make anyone else suffer for your delusions."

Cina released a long, weary sigh. "It's amusing that a handful of order-obsessed fools and children could defeat my followers with such ease. I'll grant you my respect for your skills." She chuckled. "I truly regret that you won't join my cause, Raine. You're a remarkable young woman, and your friends are impressive."

"The girl's right," Agent Oliver said. She raised her phone and waved it. "PDA reinforcements will be here in minutes. Your spell might disrupt other portals and tracking in this area, but it won't stop people from simply going to Charlottesville and then coming here without portals. We also have an FBI RRAET team en route in a dropship. You can turtle there all you want, but you're going down, you insane criminal."

"Nothing but prattle from a woman who will soon no longer exist. The enforcers think themselves the servants of righteousness, but they are fools in service to petty men with petty concerns, of those who would stop true progress." Cina raised both her hands. Bright white light spilled from her eyes, and a nimbus of silver energy surrounded her. "I applaud your efforts, but you had your chance. You will be destroyed but do not despair. Your sacrifices will join the others as the basis of a new world—a better world."

Professor Powell shouted the end of his spell. A massive twirling lance of sapphire light rocketed from his wand and exploded against her shield. It blinded everyone for a few seconds and gouged the ground to launch grass, dirt, and rock to join the cloud of smoke.

Raine held her breath. There was no way his spell didn't penetrate her defenses.

When the smoke cleared, Cina remained smiling behind her shield. "It's like I told you. It's too late for all of you. Now taste a small portion of the power I'll soon wield."

Several dark swirling portals opened in the center of the clearing.

CHAPTER THIRTY-SIX

A huge tremor shook the ground and tumbled everyone off their feet. The light from the glyphs intensified to bathe the entire clearing and nearby trees in golden light. Raine's stomach tightened, and she hissed in response. The magical pressure was overwhelming and she'd never felt anything like it.

Skittering ten-legged, four-armed crab-like creatures the size of a large dog poured from the portal in a steady line, their exoskeletons a bright fluorescent green. They ignored the fallen cultists and scuttled toward the rescue force. Stun bolts and firebolts barely slowed them. They piled to a stop near a shimmering barrier raised by Headmistress Berens and their claws ripped holes in the shield. She sealed them in an instant, but her breathing turned labored.

Head Librarian Decker and Philip disabled some of the attackers with restraint chains, but others quickly snipped the links with their massive claws as if breaking through balsa wood. Sara's kitsune entanglement spells met similar fates. The rapidly growing branches were shorn in seconds by the creatures.

"Help me," Madelyn whispered. Her voice sounded as if came from behind Raine, despite the fact that the other girl still hung in the air in the center of the clearing in front of her. "Only you can help me. Free me. Once her portals are closed, the creatures won't be able to survive. I'm connected to Cina, and I can feel how she's manipulating their energy. Remove me from here, and the ritual ends. You have to believe me."

The ground shook again and scattered a few of the crabs but knocked most of the two-legged participants to their knees. Cina remained ensconced in her shield and cloaked in energy inside, her features obscured by the bright light.

Raine hopped to her feet. "I can hear Madelyn. I need to get to her."

Cameron growled and shook his head. A small bolt of lightning cracked from Professor Powell's wand. The energy arced among the creatures and barely slowed them.

"That's not annoying at all," he said.

Agent Oliver frowned and tossed her wand into her left hand. She whipped her pistol out and opened fire. The bullets bounced off the shells in a flurry of sparks.

"Nothing we do hurts these things." She gritted her teeth. "We need to hold out until the reinforcements arrive—if not the PDA, then the RRAET team. I doubt these things can take a railgun round at point-blank range."

Raine pointed to Madelyn. "I can end it. Madelyn's the key. If I get to her, this is all over."

"How can you be so sure?" The agent looked at the sky, desperation in her eyes.

"Because Madelyn told me, and she's the one plugged into it." She pointed her wand at the scuttling horde. "Do you have any better ideas? We won't last long enough for the reinforcements."

Headmistress Berens nodded, her face ashen. "She's right. These monsters have some kind of inherent anti-magic ability. It's taking too much energy to maintain my barrier."

Another tremor shuddered, but this time, everyone managed to remain standing.

Agent Clemson sighed. "Somehow, getting ripped apart by weird crabs from another world doesn't seem like a surprising way to die. I should have been an accountant, but my dad really wanted me to join the PDA. How many accountants get ripped apart by alien crabs?"

Agent Oliver glared at him. "Stow it, Clemson."

He sighed and shrugged.

"We can survive this, and we can save Ruby Falls and Charlottesville." Head Librarian Decker nodded. "I believe in Raine."

Cameron shifted. "You know I do."

Her friends all nodded.

Professor Powell shook his head. "We'd love to help you, Raine, but we have our hands full simply holding these monsters at bay. We'd need an entire army of helpers, and then we're talking about you only having seconds to get to Madelyn."

Evie gasped and yanked a puce potion out of her pouch. "I have a mass minion potion."

The professor blinked and utter shock spread over his face. "You actually brewed a mass minion potion? I didn't think anyone actually ever made one of those except once in a blue moon as a joke."

"It was a project." She shrugged. "To reinforce technique."

"Professor Fowler's more fun than I thought."

The headmistress nodded. "Then everyone should prepare to do whatever they can to disable one of those monsters for a moment. Combined with the potion, it should be enough. Raine, you'll need to move quickly. Get ready."

She crouched and pointed her wand down. "I'll burst once it's clear." She began chanting the spell.

"Counting down from five," Headmistress Berens shouted. She stumbled as another tremor shook the area. "Five, four, three, two, one…go!"

Chains winked into existence and wrapped around several crabs. The soil turned to mud beneath others. Thick ropes plummeted from above.

Evie hurled her potion vial into the air. It tumbled end over end until it struck the ground and cracked. A brilliant flash filled the air, followed by a riot of popping sounds in rapid succession.

Earthen dolls, each a couple of feet high, burst from the soil in the hundreds and left the clearing a crater-filled mess. The minions swarmed the nearest crabs and grasped their legs. A single rip of a claw returned a doll to the pile of dirt and rock it was born from, but the sheer numbers overwhelmed the attacking creatures and distracted them.

Headmistress Berens nodded. "You're clear."

Cameron pointed. "Do what you always wanted to do, Raine. Save her."

Raine shouted the final words of the incantation of the burst spell. She hurtled forward toward Madelyn, her arms outstretched, collided with the girl, and wrapped her arms around her. Pain blasted through her body as energy flowed into her, but she held on tightly. Both girls tumbled and landed in a roll which took them past a cluster of minions. Their helpers tried to subdue several crabs and were ripped into clods for their efforts.

The portals vanished and the creatures writhed and no longer resisted the swarming dolls. Their exoskeletons hissed and vaporized in seconds, the deadly monsters now nothing more than a noxious cloud that brought tears to Raine's eyes.

She coughed and pulled Madelyn tightly against her. "It'll be okay."

Cina's shield dropped and she uttered a piercing scream. The light around her grew brighter.

Raine sat up, surrounded by swaying minions. "What's going on?"

"I was the conduit and the buffer," Madelyn said and brushed blue strands of hair out of her face. She stood and stared at the priestess. "Without me, she's overloaded with power."

Headmistress Berens deactivated her shield. The rescue force rushed over to the two girls.

"There has to be some way to save her," Raine said. Despite all the pain the woman had inflicted, it was hard to let anyone suffer and die.

Head Librarian Decker removed his bowler hat and ran his hand through his hair. "There isn't enough time."

Cina's screams stopped, and the light around her vanished. The only thing that remained was her Eye of Thoth pendant. It cracked and fell into a pile of her ashes.

"Such is the end for all those drunk on power," Professor Powell muttered and shook his head.

Agent Oliver surveyed the unconscious surviving cultists. "Let's make sure these men are secured until our reinforcements arrive. There'll be a boatload of paperwork on this, but I'm very sure the PDA will be happy we helped stop two cities from getting destroyed, even if we bent regulations a little to do it."

Agent Clemson released a sigh of relief. "I think I'll put my resignation in tomorrow."

"It's over," Raine whispered. "It's finally over." She turned to Madelyn. "You're finally free."

CHAPTER THIRTY-SEVEN

Raine frowned as Professor Powell carried the unconscious Erin toward them. The PDA agents collected wands and conjured handcuffs for their prisoners with the help of the students, but none of the cultists were conscious or aware enough to offer any resistance. From what she could tell, they had all survived, and Librarian Decker was stabilizing the severely wounded.

"There's one thing I still don't understand." Raine pointed toward Erin. "What happened, Madelyn? You obviously went to the kemana. Erin was tied up, so she wasn't working for Cina. I can't see why you of all people would leave the safety of the school." She held a palm up. "I'm not blaming you. I'm sure you had a good reason. I'm only trying to understand what it was."

Madelyn sighed. "A student delivered a note to me. They said it was from Erin. She gave it to them in the kemana. It was magically sealed, which surprised them, but they told me they thought it was 'weird Maddie magic.' And they said she acted weirdly, but they thought she was worried about getting in trouble for breaking curfew." She shook her head. "Even though she gave it to them, it wasn't from Erin. It was a threat from Cina. She didn't explain the details, but she had been watching the kemana even after your showdown, and somehow, she realized Erin was a friend of mine. She captured her and said she would kill her within an hour if I didn't come alone to the kemana." She shrugged. "I didn't have a choice. I couldn't let anyone else die for me, so I went. I didn't even put up a fight. She told me she would let Erin go, but she didn't."

Raine frowned. "But I'm your friend, too. Why spend all that time spying and waiting for Erin? She could have come after me."

"I think she was a little afraid of you in her own way after what happened last time. She even mentioned how you were 'trouble' and 'much more talented than a typical teen' before she started the ritual, and that she regretted that your talent was wasted on others instead of the Children of Thoth."

Professor Powell set Erin down gently. "You should have trusted us, Madelyn. If not us, then the Trouble Squad. This ended well, but it could have ended badly."

The Coral Elf shook her head. "I couldn't take the chance that Erin would be hurt because of me. I can't take people being hurt for me. Not again."

The headmistress shook her head. "I don't think we should encourage the students that way, Professor Powell. The last thing we want to do is encourage rogue activity."

"Soon, they won't be our students." He winked. "And that rogue activity trained them well enough that they were able to help save two cities." He pulled his wand out and cast a wake spell.

Erin's eyes fluttered open, and she looked around. "Professor Powell? Headmistress? W-what happened? Am I safe?"

"Yes, you're safe." The professor nodded. "It's all over. We're not back at the school, but we'll head there soon."

The girl sat up and looked at Madelyn. "You came for me. That woman said she would use me to get you, and I said you wouldn't come for me because it was too dangerous. Why did you come? You had to know it was a trap. She was scary."

"Yes, she was scary, but I had to come."

"Why?"

"Because you're my friend." Madelyn smiled. "That's all the reason I need."

"And the woman?"

"She's taken care of." She nodded at Raine. "Because of my other friends. She'll never bother anyone ever again."

Erin sighed and lay back on the ground. "Ugh. I'm beginning to think there's a good reason why they don't want freshmen in the kemana."

Bailey lay outside the stable door and Raine knelt to stroke his fur. She'd always found him pleasant and half-suspected the Golden Retriever was secretly an Oriceran pretending to be a dog. During her four years at the school, though, he'd never done anything other than what a person might expect a smart dog to do. Even at a magical school, a dog was sometimes simply a dog.

Horace opened the stable door and raised an auburn eyebrow. "Hello, Raine. Did you need something?" He cocked his head as if searching his memories.

She scratched Bailey behind the ears before she stood. "I wanted to know if it was okay to take Storm out for a ride."

"Really? It is fine but I'm surprised."

"Yes, I know it's been a while, but I'm graduating soon. I basically had to give him up for my FBI training, but now that I'm leaving, I've thought about the positive experiences at this school, and I want to relive those I can before I go. And I don't exactly have a lot of time." She nodded at the stable. "I was never going to be an equestrian, but that doesn't mean I didn't enjoy it and get value out of it."

"Not everything in life has to have special utility or be something you use in a future job." The groundskeeper smiled. "I still have your favorite saddle. You're welcome to ride Storm every day until you graduate if you want."

"Thank you. I might do that."

Raine stepped into the stable. The beautiful horse nickered.

Horace moved to the wall where several saddles hung. "I heard you saved us all from being blown up. That's always nice."

She laughed. "Yes, but it wasn't me. It was everyone working together—the headmistress, Professor Powell, Agent Oliver, Agent Clemson, Head Librarian Decker, and the rest of my friends, even Madelyn. As she was being drained as part of that ritual, she reached out to me. She found that strength to save herself and help save everyone."

"Friends are always nice." He lifted a saddle down. "You can do almost anything with good friends. With those and a good horse, you can drop the almost and do everything."

"I know. I've learned so much at this school, but one of the main things I've learned is that we're all so much stronger together." She accepted the saddle from him. "When I started here, it wasn't like I was a loner, but I think I was a little too obsessed with solving everything myself. Oh, well. Today's not about that. Today's about my date with a horse." She walked toward Storm's stall. "I know it's been a while, but let's have some good times these last few days."

Horace smiled warmly. "Enjoy."

CHAPTER THIRTY-EIGHT

The graduation gown was surprisingly itchy for something so loose despite the fact that she wore it over pants. Raine tapped her fingers on her knee to ease her inner restlessness and a trace of irritation. She'd always thought she had a high tolerance for speeches, but after four years of high school, her senioritis had finally kicked in. Even Headmistress Berens' stirring oratory didn't do much to move her.

It didn't matter that in a few months, she would transition directly into the FBI Academy and probably look back fondly on the easy magical education that had defined the last four years of her life. For now, she simply wanted to be done with it.

Maybe it was because graduation didn't feel like she was doing anything. It marked things she'd already done. Recognition was great, but her time at the school had further solidified her into a woman of action. Sitting around listening to more speeches didn't fit with that.

She chuckled quickly and reminded herself that she'd

experience innumerable briefings and meetings in her FBI future. If she simply thought of graduation as practice for that, it made the entire experience more palatable.

An elaborate, gleaming white stage faced rows and rows of gray metal chairs. The enchanted seats provided the appropriate resistance for almost perfect comfort for every occupant—a somewhat tedious spell that involved several of the professors putting in more than their share of night hours in the preparation for the ceremony. Making it permanent required so much effort that the chore was worth it every year.

One side of the crowd was filled with the gown-wearing graduating class. The other side was filled with friends and family. The juniors and lower sat in the rear, spread out to either side.

Raine had seen Christie near the front—not that she was easy to miss with her bright blue dress and equally bright smile. Uncle Jerry sat farther away on the other side. There had been some mild controversy about where Agent Connor would sit as he wasn't technically faculty, but in the end, he sat near the front with the professors, gnomes, and pixies.

"And now, let us recognize the achievement of the students who have worked hard for four years to master not only academics but also their magical abilities in a time of growth and difficult reflection," Headmistress Berens continued. "When I call your name, please come to the stage to receive your diploma."

For all the magic associated with the school, there was a surprising mundaneness to the graduation ceremony. True, besides the magical chairs, the headmistress used a spell instead of a microphone to magnify her voice, and a convenient magical breeze kept everyone cool, but it wasn't like they had Dorvu doing flybys and pixies delivering the diplomas. The pixies sat in tiny chairs near the front, but they played no active part in the ceremony itself.

Perhaps that was deliberate given the mixed crowd of visitors. While many of the students came from families with long magical histories, Raine wasn't the only one from a family that had only recently joined the fold. In addition, as a government-sponsored school, downplaying some of the more fantastical elements might be helpful. A visiting congressman might be a little spooked if he thought tax-payer dollars went into something too wild and Oriceran in flavor.

She thought about that for a moment. While she hadn't grown up knowing about her magic, she'd adapted so well, none of the strangeness of the school fazed her anymore. The idea that a dragon would make ice rinks for people was beyond fantastical, but it made perfect sense to her. Pixies making her meals and gnomes managing her books also felt natural and even inevitable. Perhaps the School of Necessary Magic really was a slice of Oriceran on Earth.

Her thoughts drifted through her experiences over the years as more and more students were called. Eventually, she stood and followed others, her body on autopilot.

"Raine Campbell," Headmistress Berens announced.

The student beside her poked her in the arm. She blinked, shocked at how quickly she'd been called. One minute, the headmistress began announcing graduation names, and in the next, she waited with a dozen other students near the stage.

She ascended the stairs and moved toward the headmistress, who looked elegant in her full black-and-blue professorial cap and gown. The woman handed Raine her diploma and shook her hand. Uncle Jerry's piercing whistle cut through the applause. She surveyed the crowd until she made eye contact with her guardian and he waved furiously. Her gaze found Christie next, and the perky blonde gave her a double thumbs-up. Madelyn sat too far back in the crowd for her to make eye contact.

Raine turned to leave.

"Stay here a moment, Raine." Headmistress Berens grinned.

She blinked. "O-okay."

The headmistress turned back to the crowd. "Raine is perhaps one of the single most well-known students on campus, and that's quite an achievement considering this is a campus full of strong-willed magicals. She, along with her friends, had a habit of being involved in all kinds of trouble throughout the years, and I'm not only talking about the most recent incident."

The student body erupted in laughter. Raine's cheeks burned, and she offered a sheepish grin and a shrug.

Headmistress Berens put her arm around her shoulders. "For those of you visiting parents and friends who haven't heard of Raine, she comes from a long line of FBI agents. The government has recently relaxed its policy regarding magicals serving in various positions. Accordingly, a special dispensation has been negotiated with the bureau with the help of our FBI liaison Special Agent Bruce Connor, and Raine will actually join the Academy to begin her training as the first open witch in the FBI."

The crowd erupted in cheers and applause.

"Go, Raine!" screamed one boy.

The woman waited a moment for the noise to die down. "Because of her dedication to joining the FBI and her penchant for trouble, she and her friends earned a little nickname at the school. Let's see if the students can share it with you. All at once now, please."

"*FBI Trouble Squad!*" the student body yelled in unison.

Agent Connor snickered and shook his head.

Raine took a deep breath. Embarrassment warred with pride, but her burning cheeks suggested the embarrassment was winning.

The headmistress smiled at her. "In light of your efforts to protect the School of Necessary Magic and Ruby Falls during your time here and in recognition of your status as the unofficial leader of the FBI Trouble Squad, the faculty prepared a little something for you."

She raised her hand. A crystalline statuette of what appeared to be Raine in a suit and tie winked into existence. Apparently, the headmistress was more ready to use flashy magic than the students realized. She offered the statuette to Raine, who took it and read the small plaque on the bottom.

To Raine Campbell, Leader of the FBI Trouble Squad

Most students go looking for trouble because they're bored.

Very few take care of that trouble at the risk of their own life to help others.

May you cherish your memories of your time at this school as we'll cherish our memories of you.

Headmistress Berens gestured to the crowd. "Any words for the crowd?"

Raine pointed at herself. "You want me to give a speech? I'm not the valedictorian."

"You're certainly something special." The woman smiled. "And I don't think it'd hurt to hear a few words from you."

She cleared her throat and turned toward the crowd. Her heart rate kicked up as all the eyes stared expectantly at her. She was used to public speaking from her previous experience on Student Council, but this was an entirely different order of magnitude. As she took a deep breath, she tried to remind herself that nothing all that bad could happen. The worst thing she could do was give an embarrassing speech.

"I…" She shook her head. "I don't have a lot to say. I never expected to be at this school when I was growing up because I never knew I was a magical. When my power manifested, I was dealing with bullies. I guess that makes sense. I've always been about standing up to those who want to hurt others."

Several people in the crowd nodded knowingly.

"And when I arrived here, it was overwhelming." She laughed nervously. "I was simply this normal girl for most of my life, and then one day, they tell me, 'Boom, you're a witch, and you'll go to magic school with other magicals. You'll be roommates with a kitsune and hang out with a shifter, an elf, and an Ifrit.'" She shook her head. "But you know what? The funny thing is that none of that really mattered because I quickly learned magic doesn't make that much of a difference. People are people, good and bad. Magic's only a tool.

"And yes, I got in trouble. A lot of trouble. I was raised

by parents who taught me that injustice is one of the most awful things in the world, and when I lost my parents, Uncle Jerry only reinforced that. I believed from a very young age that if I could do anything worthwhile in this world it would be to fight injustice by helping eliminate or apprehend criminals who prey on innocent people."

Uncle Jerry nodded from his seat, his tears glistening in the summer sun.

Raine licked her lips. "And I brought that same attitude to this school. Every time I ran into someone in trouble, I chose to help them—not because I had to, but because it was the right thing to do. I didn't care what they were, witch, wizard, shifter, or ferret."

"Hap rules!" someone shouted from the freshmen section.

The student body laughed.

She grinned. "The point is, many people on the friends and family side of this crowd grew up in a world where they believed magic wasn't real and there was only one intelligent species. Or so they thought. I and all my friends grew up in a world where everyone knew it wasn't true, and I thought I did, too. But I didn't, not really, until I came here and understood exactly what it means to be around other magicals.

"Now, I hope to carry that experience forward when I join the FBI and to be an example of how magicals and non-magicals can coexist for the better to make both groups stronger. Because, no matter how powerful an individual is, they are never more powerful than a group of dedicated people working together. My Trouble Squad taught me that." She teared up. "Every success I had while I was here was because I had those people at my back—people who love me and care about me." She sniffled. "And my strongest hope for any of you other students, particularly you freshman, is that you find your own Trouble Squad, even if the only trouble you get into is eating too many M&Ms at Bubble & Fizz. Cherish your time here and cherish your friends. This place is more special than you can possibly know. Take advantage of your time here. Use it to become a better person who helps those around them. The more you help other people, the more you help yourself." Raine squeezed her eyes shut and took a shuddering breath. "Thank you. I think I'm done for now."

The crowd broke out in thunderous applause. She held up her statuette and diploma and crossed hurriedly to the other side of the stage.

CHAPTER THIRTY-NINE

The students and families now mixed freely on the lawn where they chatted in small groups, shook hands, and shared hugs.

Cameron, Uncle Jerry, and Agent Connor huddled together, all laughing, apparently at something hilarious from her uncle.

"So much for keeping it mundane," Raine whispered. She snickered and realized she'd probably applied her patented Campbell overthinking to a situation that didn't warrant it.

Madelyn, who stood close to her, cocked her head, her eyes filled with curiosity. "What do you mean? What's mundane?"

She gestured toward the sky. "I thought they would try to keep this a little low-key, but it's hard to be low-key with a dragon flying around."

Dorvu circled overhead. Upon reflection, perhaps there weren't that many people in the crowd not already thoroughly comfortable with magic. Or maybe the staff didn't feel the need for flashy magic to impress a group of people already familiar with magic. She felt sudden pity for people who were event planners before the gates began to open and could only imagine having to compete with people with direct access to magic.

A mischievous smile slid over Madelyn's face. "Low key? That won't happen."

"Why? Do you know something I don't?"

The Coral Elf nodded. "There's a surprise the headmistress arranged. It involves all the underclassmen. It'll definitely not be low key." She looked off into the distance. "Erin's waving at me for some reason. Is it okay if I go talk to her?"

"Yes, go ahead. We can talk later. I won't leave this place without a few scheduled visits with you."

The girl waved and hurried toward her roommate in the distance.

Jillian maneuvered through a thick section of the crowd and strolled toward Raine, a huge smile on her face. She extended her hand. "It was a good speech, Raine. I could have made a better one, but it was still a good speech. Your talents might be wasted in the FBI."

She shook Jillian's hand. "Thanks, I think."

"You're welcome." The Gray Elf gave her a curt nod and wandered off.

Sara waved her arms at her grandmother and pointed into the distance. The old kitsune turned, and her granddaughter ran in the opposite direction toward Raine.

She pulled her friend into a hug. "I don't know what I'll do without you getting me into trouble." Her cheeks were already puffy from near-constant tears. "My life will be so boring and non-dangerous without you around me every day."

Raine pulled away with a grin. "Don't worry. I'll visit you and make sure mobsters are following me, or—I don't know, James Brownstone or something. I'm sure he can blow up a building or two."

Sara laughed. She pointed to Philip and his family in the distance. "I need to put in an appearance, but I'll catch up with you later."

"Sure. I'll wander past to say hi to Philip, too."

The kitsune nodded and waved before she headed toward her boyfriend and his family.

Raine wandered away from Cameron, Uncle Jerry, and Agent Connor. She let the event wash over her and simply smiled and enjoyed the happy faces in the crowd. So many people mingled, united in the joy of a shared Rite of Passage. She believed what she'd said in her speech and suspected she wouldn't feel differently at a regular high school graduation.

She offered handshakes and congratulations here and there. Juniper and Malcolm, Georgina, and countless others she'd befriended or shared classes with. Her meandering path eventually brought her to Evie and William. She gave them both quick hugs before she caught sight of Professor Powell and Head Librarian Decker across the field.

"Hey, I'll catch up with you in a few minutes," she said. "I just wanted to go say hello to Professor Powell. It might be harder to catch some of the staff afterward."

Evie smiled. "We're not going anywhere anytime soon,

Raine. You have to understand how slow my family is when it comes to ceremony. If we get out of here today, I'd be surprised."

Raine laughed. "Heard and understood." She squeezed her friend's shoulder before heading over to where the two staff members were absorbed in conversation. "Hello, Professor, Head Librarian."

Professor Powell extended his hand. "You're not a student anymore. How about you call me Xander so I don't have to call you Agent Campbell later?"

The head librarian's poppy blew a raspberry. He tapped it before he smiled. "And I think you've long since earned the right to call me Leo."

"To be honest, it feels weird." She shrugged.

Both men grinned.

"Okay, Xander, Leo." She laughed. "I bet you won't miss me, Xander. You're the unofficial head of security here, it seems, and I know me and the Squad created considerable trouble for you."

Xander snickered. "My mere existence creates trouble." His easy smile faded into a more serious look. "And no, I'll miss you greatly. You're the embodiment of the kind of student I want to teach. It's easy to have a powerful magical come in and display their raw power, but you're a person who mastered your skills through dedication and hard work. That is why you've been able to face powerful opponents, despite being a student. I don't know if I can put into words how proud I was of the entire Trouble Squad with Cina. You weren't students there. You might as well have been experienced PDA agents."

She averted her eyes. "We weren't that good."

"Yes, you were." He grinned. "And trust me, I know a thing or two about dealing with dangerous witches and wizards. It wasn't only your technique but your discipline. Many people don't remain calm when their lives are in danger, Raine. That's not something you can teach. It's something people have to develop themselves from experience, but yes, I'll definitely miss you. I like almost all my students, but I won't lie and say I don't have a few favorites."

"I'll miss you, too, of course," Leo said. "And I'm unabashed in admitting favoritism. It's rare that I encounter a student with such a healthy respect for the written word and knowledge. If even a tenth of the students at this school cared as much about pure self-improvement as you did, the future would be grand indeed. My library won't be the same. It'll feel so empty—it already felt sad when you started spending less time in there."

Raine sighed. "I'm sorry."

The gnome shook his head. "Don't be. You used that time to become a better FBI trainee. You also never disrespected my library or books, and I know you'll be a fine FBI witch. I also know you'll continue to make us proud, whether in the agency or if you decide to become a scholar later."

"Exactly." Xander adjusted his cap. "Now, if you'll excuse me, Raine. I do need to have a short discussion with a few parents who had some complaints about some aspects of my teaching style." He grinned and wandered off.

"He plans to argue with someone at a graduation?"

Leo shrugged. "That's the best time to do it. In many cases, the parents might not be someone you'll ever see again."

Raine looked down at the head librarian. "I know we've talked about it before, but this really doesn't hurt? I mean, I..." She shook her head. "I can't imagine being hundreds of years old and having so many comings and goings."

"It's because you're young that it hurts, Raine. When you grow older, you'll learn to appreciate the flow of life for what it is. I'm not ecstatic when my favorite students leave, but I understand that it's part of the cycle of existence."

"Cycle of existence?" Headmistress Berens interjected from behind her. "Such heady conversation. This is supposed to be a time of celebration and fun."

He bobbed his head. "You should see the kind of books Raine reads for fun. This is light material compared to those."

Raine turned and shook the headmistress's hand.

The woman smiled. "I hope I didn't upset you too much with my little ambush on stage."

She shook her head. "I was emotional because of all the memories, not over having to give the speech."

"I understand. I look forward to following your long and fruitful career." Headmistress Berens nodded to Xander in the distance. He grinned at a frowning man who shook a finger in his face. "If you want to come back in a couple of decades, maybe Xander will let you co-teach defense against dark magic. I'm sure you'll have considerable practical experience."

"I don't really see myself as a professor, but I'll keep that in mind."

The woman nodded. "You've been a pleasure, Raine, even when you were frustrating." She nodded approvingly and moved toward another student and their family.

After excusing herself from Leo, Raine headed toward her own family and waved at Adrien and Christie who chatted with his parents and older brother. Before she could make it back to Uncle Jerry, Cameron jogged over to her.

"Where did you disappear to?" he asked.

"Oh, I made the rounds. I know I can keep in contact with people once we get away from all these wards, but it's still a little overwhelming to realize I've graduated."

He pulled her into a hug and patted her back. "If it's ever overwhelming, all you have to do is let me help carry your burden."

"I know," she said softly.

The shifter stepped back. "We should spend the summer together. The entire thing. We won't have that time again for a while between college and the FBI Academy. Maybe a month or so in Michigan and then a month with my pack before you prepare to wander off to Quantico."

"It sounds like a good idea." Raine took a few deep breaths. "Sorry. I'm trying not to start crying again."

"Excuse me, everyone," Headmistress Berens announced and her voice seemed to come from all directions. "The other non-graduating classes have a little surprise to share with the graduating class."

"Madelyn mentioned this," Raine said. "Why didn't we

have a special surprise for the graduating classes the last few years?"

Cameron shrugged. "Who knows? Traditions change."

"Everyone, get ready," the headmistress said.

Dorvu stopped his overflights and suddenly soared toward the stables.

The freshmen, sophomores, and juniors all drew wands or raised their arms, depending on their species.

"Three, two, one," Headmistress Berens said.

Hundreds of spells launched at once. Orbs leaving fiery trails soared into the sky and exploded in a swarm to form a hanging garden of flame and light. It was impressive, even in broad daylight. Some of them released dozens of smaller spheres and each disappeared in a crackle and puff of light and smoke. Others exploded with visible shockwaves of different colors. The students launched a second wave to fill the sky again, but after a few seconds, the smoke coalesced into a message.

Happy Graduation!

Raine laughed. "That's cool."

Cameron wrapped an arm around her shoulders. "So, do you feel different now? Does having the ceremony make any difference?"

"Yes, I do feel different." She nodded slowly. "Because I am different. I came here a girl, and I'm leaving as a witch."

The End

Raine's adventures at the School of Necessary Magic are over. Who knows where the future will take her...

If you enjoyed her story, be sure to check out other series releasing later this year, including The Witch Next Door, Dwarf Bounty Hunter, *and more releases in* The Last Vampire *and* Federal Agents of Magic *series.*

FREE BOOKS!

 **WARNING: The Troll is now in charge.**
And he's giving away free books if you sign-up!

Join the only newsletter hosted by a Troll!

Get sneak peeks, exclusive giveaways, behind the scenes content, and more.
PLUS you'll be notified of special **one day only fan pricing** on new releases.

CLICK HERE

or visit: https://marthacarr.com/read-free-stories/

DARK IS HER NATURE

For Hire: Teachers for special school in Virginia countryside.

Must be able to handle teenagers with special abilities.

Cannot be afraid to discipline werewolves, wizards, elves and other assorted hormonal teens.

Apply at the School of Necessary Magic.

<u>**AVAILABLE ON AMAZON RETAILERS AND IN KINDLE UNLIMITED!**</u>

THE PEABRAIN'S IDEA

Find the compass, save the world or save herself?

Dating is harder for Maggie Parker than running down a felon. Now add in magic.

Did she just see a compass fly?

Can she learn how to use the magic of bubbles to chart a new course in time? It's a lot harder than it sounds.

Join her on her quest to rescue passengers on an ancient ship – a big blue marble called Earth – and save herself.

AVAILABLE ON AMAZON AND IN KINDLE UNLIMITED!

AUTHOR NOTES - MARTHA CARR

JULY 2, 2019

When I started doing these author notes I started out trying to be funny all the time. I mean, I read Anderle's notes and they're simple, a brief picture of his day and hilarious. I wanted that. On top of that I read the Offspring's drive by comments on Facebook and thought, yeah, smart funny, even harder. I want that. Then, I see Craig Martelle's one liners that point out the absurd so well without being mean, and I ponder, wouldn't that be nice if that could be me?

But then I learn something all over again. I have to be true to myself. It's the only way these things work. I'm more of an observer on life that can point out the funny, but mixed in is the vulnerable, the aspirational and the desire to connect. If I made you laugh and then pause to think about it, that's perfect.

I like to say I write recess – it's mean to take you away to somewhere else, make you laugh, get your heart going and have you join in someone's romance – and maybe go back to your world feeling a little better about everything Tall order, I know.

I was born an optimist looking for a reason to believe in everything. My father used to say that if I was given a box of manure I'd search to the bottom for the pony. All true. Mixed in is a love of people and especially anyone who's different because they're creative or have a different perspective on things in general or has a dream they're determined to follow.

I can remember being like this from the day I showed up. It makes for an interesting life and starts to explain why I like to write in urban fantasy so much. It also informs what kind of characters I write. They care about the people who are around them. They believe in solutions and don't focus on the problems (that's life changing when you can make that one small switch). They're courageous and honest and are fiercely loyal to those around them. And they're funny and vulnerable and searching to conquer an outer quest and an inner one. Often, it's how to connect more deeply with others around them.

I'm also a big fan of popular culture and love to throw in the more odd reference that everyone would still get but doesn't hear as often. And the slow burn kind of romance that makes you fall in love and ache with both characters and feel like it happened to you by the time they finally come together. And root for them as they join forces to conquer the monsters out there.

I hope you enjoyed the last story in this series and from The School of Necessary Magic! There's more fun coming this summer and maybe even a few old favorites.

Stay tuned. More recess on its way – And more adventures to follow.

AUTHOR NOTES - MICHAEL ANDERLE

JULY 7, 2019

THANK YOU for not only reading this story but these *Author Notes* as well.

(I think I've been good with always opening with "thank you." If not, I need to edit the other *Author Notes*!)

RANDOM (*sometimes*) THOUGHTS?

New Jersey (driving down the Jersey Turnpike from NY) is very pretty. The cutout to get gas and food / snacks was cool and frankly, my first time back in NJ after 20 years was enjoyable.

Not what I expected.

Unfortunately, New Jersey has a bad reputation as a state from both those who live in New York (expected) and those who live in New Jersey (not exactly expected and a whole lot more believable.)

Sorry New Yorkers.

Now, my only review of New Jersey this trip was down the turnpike and the area on the river separating New

Jersey from Pennsylvania. The area reminded me (a lot) of the area in California in the mountains near Lake Arrowhead / Big Bear. Lots and lots of trees and winding roads.

Just without the 5,000 foot drop off the side of the mountain and KERSPLAT at the bottom.

Although I did have to go across one metal bridge that was so narrow, it had me sucking in my stomach when we passed another car.

As if me sucking in my stomach did jack-all for the width of the car I was driving... (spoiler: it does not.)

When I saw a larger SUV drive onto the bridge (it was about 70 yards across I'm guessing) I was cursing up a storm in my mind.

I hadn't considered how I would react on the way back across the bridge when it was dark outside.

That sucked.

Other than that, this area in south NJ near Longhorn, Pennsylvania is beautiful.

(But I totally get why ghost stories would be popular subjects to write about if you lived here.)

AROUND THE WORLD IN 80 DAYS

One of the interesting (at least to me) aspects of my life is the ability to work from anywhere and at any time. In the future, I hope to re-read my own *Author Notes* and remember my life as a diary entry.

Yeardly, Pennsylvania / New Jersey border.

As I mentioned, I'm in this neck of the woods. I'm here for a wedding of my wife's really good friend and her new husband. (Or him and his new wife... What's proper here?)

Either way, it was a FUN event and really beautiful. The wedding was held in the backyard, about 10 yards away from Sherwood Forest (the concept, not England) and the rain started at 5:30pm and went until at least 6:30 or later.

I loved it.

The rain hit the large tent we were under and was soothing. The only cataclysmic situation was the bar was about 50 feet away through the rain.

I had to go for it (that was were the Coke was being stashed.)

I told my wife I was heading over there. She told me I needed an umbrella. I looked at her funny, asking why that was a problem.

"It's raining."

"I shower, except this time it will be with clothes on."

I don't think she ever understood my logic.

I have two arms and two hands like a normal human, nothing more and nothing less. When I ask her if she wanted anything as I was going regardless of rain, she asked for some fruity red drink. I was about to step manly across the grass as the heavens opened and released their best shower yet.

Then, my wife asked the lady next to her if she would like something.

The smile stayed on my face, but inside my head I was cussing up a storm. Not because she asked (that was the polite thing to do) but because of the comment above.

I only have *two hands*.

I make it across the storm of the century (total lie - but

not by too much) and reach the bar, under the tiny tent that allowed about 18" of space between dry and waterfall. I finish filling the two red fruity wine drinks and ask for a Coke.

The bartender starts looking around, and pulls out a Coke in a can. SCORE! I'm totally going to be able to slip that can into my pocket, and one trip this.

Then, before I can say a word, he's opened the can, grabbed a cup, dropped ice in and started pouring my can of Coke into it.

I start cursing in my mind again.

I blew out my frustration, walked through the hurricane back to the big tent and delivered the two drinks.

Then, I turned around and gave the post-apocalyptic rain the mental finger as I went back to get my Coke.

Because THAT was what I wanted in the first place and real men don't @#!#% melt in the rain.

But we do deliver our wives drinks first.

FAN PRICING

$0.99 Saturdays (new LMBPN stuff) and $0.99 Wednesday (both LMBPN books and friends of LMBPN books.) Get great stuff from us and others at tantalizing prices.

Go ahead, I bet you can't read just one.

Sign up here: http://lmbpn.com/email/.

HOW TO MARKET FOR BOOKS YOU LOVE

Review them so others have your thoughts, tell friends

and the dogs of your enemies (because who wants to talk with enemies?)... *Enough said ;-)*

Ad Aeternitatem,

Michael Anderle

OTHER SERIES IN THE ORICERAN UNIVERSE:

SCHOOL OF NECESSARY MAGIC
SCHOOL OF NECESSARY MAGIC: RAINE CAMPBELL
ALISON BROWNSTONE
THE DANIEL CODEX SERIES
THE LEIRA CHRONICLES
I FEAR NO EVIL
FEDERAL AGENTS OF MAGIC
THE UNBELIEVABLE MR. BROWNSTONE
REWRITING JUSTICE
THE KACY CHRONICLES
MIDWEST MAGIC CHRONICLES
SOUL STONE MAGE
THE FAIRHAVEN CHRONICLES

OTHER BOOKS BY JUDITH BERENS

OTHER BOOKS BY MARTHA CARR

OTHER SERIES IN THE ORICERAN UNIVERSE:

JOIN THE ORICERAN UNIVERSE FAN GROUP ON FACEBOOK!

BOOKS BY MICHAEL ANDERLE

For a complete list of books by Michael Anderle, please visit

www.lmbpn.com/ma-books/

All LMBPN Audiobooks are Available at Audible.com and iTunes. For a complete list of audiobooks visit:

www.lmbpn.com/audible

CONNECT WITH THE AUTHORS

Martha Carr Social

Website: http://www.marthacarr.com

Facebook: https://www.facebook.com/groups/MarthaCarrFans/

Michael Anderle Social

Michael Anderle Social Website:
http://www.lmbpn.com

Email List:
http://lmbpn.com/email/

Facebook Here: https://www.facebook.com/TheKurtherianGambitBooks/

www.ingramcontent.com/pod-product-compliance
Lightning Source LLC
LaVergne TN
LVHW041623060526
838200LV00040B/1414